Praise for Vicki Lewis Thompson

"Thompson continues to do what she does best, tying together strong family values bound by blood and choice, interspersed with the more sizzling aspects of the relationship."

—*RT Book Reviews* on *Thunderstruck*

"All the characters, background stories and character development are positively stellar; the warm family feeling is not saccharine-sweet, but heartfelt and genuine, and Lexi and Cade's rekindled romance is believable from beginning to end, along with the classy, sexy and tender love scenes."

—*Fresh Fiction* on *Midnight Thunder*

"Intensely romantic and hot enough to singe...her Sons of Chance series never fails to leave me worked up from all the heat, and then sighing with pleasure at the happy endings!"

—*We Read Romance* on *Riding High*

"If I had to use one word to describe *Ambushed!* it would be *charming*... Where the story shines and how it is elevated above others is the humor that is woven throughout."

—*Dear Author*

"The chemistry between Molly and Ben is off the charts: their first kiss is one of the best I've ever read, and the sex is blistering a̶̶̶̶̶t respectful, tender and loving."

—̶̶̶̶ *A Last Chance Christmas*

"*Cowboy Up* is̶̶̶̶̶̶̶̶̶̶̶̶̶̶̶̶̶̶ d̶-
natured humo̶̶̶̶̶̶̶̶̶̶̶̶̶̶̶̶̶̶̶̶ail.
Another sizzli̶̶̶̶̶̶̶̶̶̶̶̶̶̶̶̶̶̶̶̶ Choice
Award winner ̶̶̶̶̶̶̶̶̶̶̶̶̶̶̶̶̶̶̶̶̶̶̶̶̶̶̶̶̶̶̶̶̶̶̶̶ *Reviews*

Dear Reader,

Oh, those Magee brothers! In *Cowboy After Dark*, I fell in love with Liam and figured his younger brother Grady couldn't possibly be as endearing. Was I ever wrong! Please don't ask me to pick my favorite Magee brother. I doubt you'll be able to, either, after you meet Grady, the cowboy turned metal artist. I guarantee he's hotter than a blowtorch!

Like Sapphire Ferguson, I have a weakness for creative men because they're creative in...well, everything they do, if you get my meaning. Grady's sculptures of majestic creatures like eagles and wolves are crafted with recycled metal, which makes him both artistic and ecologically aware! Not only that, but he gets hot and sweaty doing it. Sculpting, that is. What did you think I was talking about?

Okay, I don't blame you for going there. The minute you get a glimpse of this tall cowboy with his muscles and slightly shaggy haircut, you'll be ready to trade places with Sapphire. And when you find out Grady's plan to make a sculpture for Rosie, his foster mom, your heart is gonna melt.

Welcome back to the Thunder Mountain Brotherhood! This amazing band of men each experienced a tragedy that landed them in foster care, but they were all lucky enough to find a home with Rosie and Herb at Thunder Mountain Ranch. Their days at the ranch taught them the cowboy way and forged an enduring bond, although love doesn't come easily to guys with emotional scars. Join me for another story featuring the awesome cowboys who call themselves the Thunder Mountain Brotherhood!

Creatively yours,

Vicki Lewis Thompson

Vicki Lewis Thompson

Cowboy Untamed

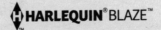
HARLEQUIN® BLAZE™

ISBN-13: 978-0-373-79907-7

Cowboy Untamed

Printed in U.S.A.

www.Harlequin.com

A passion for travel has taken *New York Times* bestselling author **Vicki Lewis Thompson** to Europe, Great Britain, the Greek isles, Australia and New Zealand. She's visited most of North America and has her eye on South America's rain forests. Africa, India and China beckon. But her first love is her home state of Arizona, with its deserts, mountains, sunsets and—last but not least—cowboys! The wide-open spaces and heroes on horseback influence everything she writes. Connect with her at vickilewisthompson.com, Facebook.com/vickilewisthompson and Twitter.com/vickilthompson.

Books by Vicki Lewis Thompson

Harlequin Blaze

Thunder Mountain Brotherhood

Midnight Thunder
Thunderstruck
Rolling Like Thunder
A Cowboy Under the Mistletoe
Cowboy All Night
Cowboy After Dark

Sons of Chance

Cowboys & Angels
Riding High
Riding Hard
Riding Home
A Last Chance Christmas

To get the inside scoop on Harlequin Blaze and its talented writers, be sure to check out BlazeAuthors.com.

All backlist available in ebook format.

Visit the Author Profile page at Harlequin.com for more titles.

To visual artists—dedicated souls who enrich our lives by allowing us to see the world through their eyes.

1

A WYOMING SUNSET tinged the horizon pale orange, reminding Grady Magee of the Dreamsicles he used to crave as a kid. But thoughts of adult pleasures nudged out childhood nostalgia as he parked his truck in front of the Sheridan Art Barn next to a grape-colored pickup, the only other vehicle in the lot. It likely belonged to Sapphire Ferguson, the woman who'd been on his mind during most of the long drive from Cody.

Three weeks ago during a visit to Thunder Mountain Ranch, he'd come by here with his foster brother Cade to pick up some local art for Cade's new cabin. Sapphire, a talented potter, had been minding the store. He'd barely recognized her.

The quiet girl he remembered from high school had morphed into a confident woman with a smoldering glance that set him on fire. When she'd asked him to headline a charity event featuring artists creating work on the spot, he'd set aside his packed schedule and agreed without finding out what the charity was. Didn't matter.

Hauling his tools and materials from Cody and setting up a studio in a corner of this renovated barn was a pain in the ass. He didn't care. Sapphire had his attention. While honing his welding skills in Alaska and dreaming of making a living with recycled metal art, he'd also dreamed of the kind of woman he'd want to share his life with.

She'd be a self-starter, imaginative, bold and sensual. Good looks wouldn't hurt but sexual chemistry was more important. Getting both would be a bonus. In short, the woman of his dreams was a lot like Sapphire Ferguson. Maybe his first impression would turn out to be wrong. Or maybe she already had someone in her life.

His gut told him she didn't. She wasn't wearing a ring and she'd acted as fascinated with him as he'd been with her. Since then, they'd communicated only through brief phone texts because they'd both battled crazy deadlines. He could be imagining the hum of sexual energy underlying those texts, but he didn't think so.

He climbed out of his truck with that same energy fizzing in his veins. She'd agreed to meet him and help him get his stuff unloaded, but he hadn't counted on being alone with her. Eight other artists were part of the co-op Sapphire had organized, each claiming one of the renovated stalls as both a work and display space. He'd expected some of them to be around.

Apparently, they weren't as manic about working as he was. He put in long hours, both because he loved it and because the commissions kept coming and he didn't like making customers wait. His brother Liam had reminded him that building a successful career in less than three years was unusual and few artists made a living, let alone a good living.

Grady believed him, although he didn't have much to go on. He'd used the nest egg he'd saved during his pipeline job to keep him afloat while he followed his dream. His first sculptures had sold like hotcakes and after that he'd been so busy keeping up with the demand that he'd had no time to hang out with other artists.

Spending time with Sapphire was his primary motivation for doing the charity event, but he also looked forward to conversations with other creative types. Not to say he was disappointed that he and Sapphire were alone tonight. Fraternizing with the other co-op members could wait.

He'd started toward the double-door entrance when he heard a woman's soft voice coming from somewhere to the right of the barn. He couldn't make out the words, but from the sound of it she really liked the person she was talking to. He paused to listen. Maybe he had this all wrong and the grape-colored pickup had brought two people here—Sapphire and her boyfriend. That would suck.

Standing very still, he listened for a response, a deeper murmur that would indicate she was with a guy. Nothing. He edged closer so he could make out what she was saying.

"Come on, Fred," she crooned. "You know you want this."

Dear God. If Sapphire was about to have sex with someone named Fred up against the side of the barn, he did *not* want to be here. Yeah, he'd arrived a little earlier than planned because he'd broken a few speed limits on the way. She might not be expecting him for another hour.

"You liked it last night, remember? Don't be shy."

Grady squeezed his eyes shut. This couldn't be happening. He'd pinned his hopes on Sapphire being available, yet he'd had no proof of that. If he stayed here much longer, he'd find out exactly how misguided his assumptions were.

Better to quietly climb back into his truck and slowly exit the parking lot. If they were about to get busy, they wouldn't hear him drive away. He'd grab a cup of coffee in the diner.

"There you go. Isn't that nice?"

Yikes. He took a slow step backward, then another.

"Such a good boy. Such a brave kitty-cat."

Kitty-cat? He froze. No man with an ounce of self-respect would let a woman call him *kitty-cat.* And now that he thought about it, no straight guy would need coaxing in order to have sex with a woman like Sapphire.

He crept to the corner of the building to take a look and discovered Sapphire crouched in the dry grass, the golden glow of the sunset igniting sparks of fire in her long auburn hair. She'd placed several bowls in a semi-circle around her and he counted eleven cats munching away. Instead of having sex, she was feeding strays.

He sighed in relief. The sound wasn't loud but it caught everyone's attention. Sapphire and all eleven cats looked at him. A black cat with white markings backed away from the dish. "Sorry," Grady muttered.

She kept her voice low. "You're early."

"Traffic was light."

"You'd better not come any closer. I'd like Fred to eat some more."

"Fred." He swallowed so he wouldn't laugh and spook the cats.

"Fred Astaire. The tuxedo. He's the most skittish of the bunch but I'm making progress with him."

Grady had never heard anyone refer to a cat as a *tuxedo* but it was a great description. The white patch on Fred's chest made him look as if he'd dressed for the Oscars.

All the cats went back to eating except Fred. Hunkered down, eyes wide and pupils dilated, he stared at Grady. His whiskers, white to match his chest, trembled.

"He won't hurt you, sweetie." Sapphire's voice dripped honey as she spoke to the cat. "The food's yum-yum-yummy, kitty-cat. You know you want some. Come on, come and get it."

Her words seemed to have no effect on Fred but they were having a definite effect on Grady. After three weeks of erotic dreams featuring her in the lead role, he was a hot mess of raging hormones. Listening to her woo the cat was initiating action below his belt. She'd told him to stay put but that could prove embarrassing if she kept up this seductive murmur. Sure, she was addressing a cat, but he had no trouble imagining her using that same tone during sex. The longer he stood there, the larger his problem grew, so to speak.

He couldn't very well tell her that. "Maybe I should move so Fred can't see me." He hoped she hadn't heard the telltale huskiness in his voice.

"That might help." Fortunately, she didn't glance over at him. "I'll be finished in a few minutes."

"I'll meet you out front." He began a slow retreat, wincing at the pressure of his zipper against his pride and joy.

"Okay." She went back to sweet-talking Fred.

He did his best to block the sound as he ducked out of sight and made the painful journey to his truck. Bracing both hands on the hood, he took several deep breaths. Anyone would think he was some horny teenager.

Normally, he didn't have this issue. He thought back to the last woman he'd dated and was shocked to realize they'd broken up more than a year ago. Time flew when you were making art. She'd never understood his preoccupation with his work and they'd fought about it enough times that they'd decided to call it quits last July.

Okay, so he hadn't been in bed with a woman for a long time and now he'd found someone so hot that he'd fixated on her for weeks. That could explain his sudden stiffy. He felt a little better about his reaction, although he'd have to watch himself to make sure he didn't come across as sex starved.

Turning around, he leaned his butt against the truck and adjusted himself. Better now. He repositioned his new Stetson so it sat more firmly on his head. Liam had talked him into buying it to fit his image as a celebrated Western artist and it was the most expensive one he'd ever owned—black with a silver-and-turquoise hatband. Naturally, Liam had insisted such a hat deserved a new pair of boots, also black, with fancy stitching. Grady had worn them to make a good impression but he'd brought his old scuffed ones to work in.

He had two projects in mind. First he would put together a nice sculpture for his foster mom, Rosie Padgett. She and his foster dad, Herb, had welcomed Grady and Liam to Thunder Mountain Ranch ten years ago when their mom's car accident had left her unable to care for a couple of rowdy teens. Last month Rosie had hinted to Liam that she'd love a sculpture, and Grady had come up with a great idea for the design.

Creating Rosie's gift would help him settle into the workspace, so he'd be ready to put on a performance for the charity night. He'd come up with a sketch for that one, too, and it was a piece he could finish within the three hours allotted to the event. Sapphire planned to have a silent auction for his contribution and she hoped to raise a lot of money.

He really should find out what the charity was. His sculpture should relate to the cause in some way, and just because he liked the cougar he'd sketched, didn't mean it would work with the evening's theme. He'd ask Sapphire about that when she finished feeding the stray cats. It was possible she'd told him and the information hadn't registered, because he'd been so focused on her.

Nudging his hat back with his thumb, he gazed up as the first stars blinked on. They weren't as bright in town as they were out at the ranch. Much as he'd love to stay with his foster parents during his time in Sheridan, it wasn't practical.

Thunder Mountain Academy, a new venture that involved teaching high school kids about everything related to horses, was in its last week of the summer session. The cabins that had once housed foster boys were now filled with teens enrolled in the program. Grady would only be in the way, so he'd accepted an offer to stay in town with Ben and Molly Radcliffe.

Ben had made saddles for just about everyone Grady knew in Sheridan, including his foster parents. Molly was Cade Gallagher's cousin, although Grady hadn't quite worked out the details of that connection. It had something to do with the well-known Chance brothers in Jackson Hole. In any case, Molly and Ben were part of the Thunder Mountain Ranch extended family and they were happy to let him use their guest room.

He'd warned them he didn't know when he'd show up. Unloading his equipment and materials had to come first. At least, that was how he'd rationalized stopping at the Art Barn to meet with Sapphire. Technically, he could have driven over to Molly and Ben's tonight and brought his supplies here in the morning.

Yet when he'd suggested stopping by tonight to drop them off, Sapphire had readily agreed. Her eagerness had fired up his imagination, and discovering that she was here alone added to the anticipation. He wondered if she'd had dinner. He ran through the restaurant options and decided to suggest his favorite bar because it had live music and a dance floor.

"That takes care of that." Sapphire rounded the corner of the barn holding a stack of bowls. "I thought I'd be done before you got here."

He pushed himself away from the truck and walked toward her. "No worries. Do you feed them every night?" She looked even prettier than he remembered—wavy auburn hair pulled back on one side with an elaborate silver comb, exotic earrings that dangled to her shoulders, a low-cut peasant blouse and a brightly patterned skirt that reminded him of gypsies.

"We feed them every night and every morning. We rotate weeks and this happens to be mine." She tipped her head toward the double doors at the entrance. "Come on in. I need to wash these and then I'll help you unload your equipment."

"Thanks. That would be great." He caught the spicy scent of her perfume, the same one she'd worn when they'd met three weeks ago. He breathed it in and all his hopes and dreams came flooding back. "So everyone pitches in to feed the strays?" He wondered if she liked to dance. Even if she wasn't much for dancing, they could get out on the floor and do the shuffle-and-sway routine to a slow tune so he could hold her.

"They're not exactly strays. Can you please catch the door for me?"

"Sure thing." He hurried to do it, berating himself as he slid the barn door open. He'd been so busy making plans for tonight that he'd forgotten his manners.

"You can check out the new pieces on display while I wash these."

"You have a sink?"

"During the renovation we put in a small bathroom and a tiny kitchen." She gestured toward the row of stalls. "Go ahead and look around. I left on the lights so you could see the new stuff. Everyone's getting ready for the big weekend. Lots of good work."

"Sounds great, but I'd be glad to help you with the cat dishes." Even in high school he'd been fascinated by her turquoise eyes. He'd never asked her out, because he'd been busy denying his own artistic leanings. He'd had a feeling she could see who he really was and he hadn't been ready to acknowledge that yet.

She smiled. "It's a one-person job. Go ahead and browse."

"Okay." But he sure hated to leave those eyes and that smile. He thought about both as he walked down the aisle between the stalls. Although he glanced at the artwork along the way, all he really cared about tonight was Sapphire's pottery.

Three weeks ago Cade had bought a vase of hers that Grady would have given his eyeteeth for. But the trip had been for Cade and so he'd scored the vase. Grady was curious as to what else she'd added to her collection since then.

Her display was conveniently located next to the large stall that would be his for the next several days. He stepped into the space and sucked in a breath. During his first visit here he'd noticed the sensuality of her work, and the newest pieces were even more dramatic, especially her dinnerware set.

The saturated colors and undulating lines of the single place setting made him wonder what sort of orgy the two of them could have with food served on these dishes. Picking up a red bowl with a dark purple interior, he cradled it in both hands and ran his thumb over the pebbled rim. The bowl was a tactile and visual feast.

Her potter's wheel stood in the corner ready for the next project, and he wanted to be there to see if her expression while creating was as passionate as the work itself. If she'd had an erotic nature back in high school, he'd totally missed the clues.

Not surprising. He'd been an insecure idiot back then, but he'd changed and so had she. He'd embraced his true calling and had finally realized that testosterone and art weren't mutually exclusive. Obviously, she'd grown out of her timid phase.

"That collection's new."

He turned to find her standing in the opening that used to be the stall door. He'd been absorbed in his plans and hadn't heard her footsteps. "It's sexy."

"You're not the first person who seems to feel that way." Her gaze met his and for a moment there was a flash of heat. Then she looked away and studied the colorful dinnerware. "I put that place setting out yesterday and I can already tell it startles people."

"Why?" His blood warmed as he registered the interest he'd seen in her eyes. This could turn into an excellent evening.

"The colors seem to make them nervous. They're also thrown for a loop when I explain that each place setting's slightly different. Most people expect their dinner dishes to match. It'll take a certain kind of customer."

Like me. But buying her pottery right off the bat might brand him as a suck-up. He would get some eventually and, if everything turned out the way he'd like it to, they'd enjoy a meal together, preferably naked.

He gestured toward the wheel. "You obviously work here."

"Yep. I visualized this as a combination studio and gallery from the beginning. Not everyone spends as much time here as I do, but I love it. The concrete floor is easy to clean and nobody cares if it gets stained. I have a kiln out back. Best conditions I've ever had."

"The venue makes a difference." He glanced at the large stall where he'd be setting up. "Looks like we'll be neighbors."

"Uh-huh. I like being in the back. Earlier this summer I considered moving into what'll be your space but I didn't, which is a good thing. Ready to unload your truck?"

"You bet." He set the bowl down with great care. His work was nearly indestructible but hers could be a victim of gravity. He didn't want that on his conscience.

He hauled in the big stuff—odd pieces of scrap metal and unusual gears and machine parts that he scavenged from anywhere he could find them. The hunt was part of the fun, although he didn't have as much time for it as he used to. Friends had volunteered to comb junkyards for him and Liam was always on the lookout for interesting finds.

Sapphire carried in a box of welding equipment. "Where do you want this?" She stood in the middle of the spacious stall with her arms full.

"In the corner's okay for now. I'll set up everything tomorrow. Have you had dinner?"

"Um, no." She put the box down and turned back to him. Instead of looking eager, she seemed wary. "But I'd planned to head home and catch up on some paperwork."

Not the response he was hoping for. "How about taking some time to grab a bite with me at Scruffy's Bar? There are a few things I'd like to discuss."

Her expression remained guarded. "I guess I could. I'll meet you over there, but I can't stay long."

"That's fine." It wasn't fine at all. Where was that spark he'd seen a moment ago? He'd pictured her falling right in with his plan. They'd have a few drinks, dance a little and explore what he'd hoped would be a mutual attraction.

Maybe she had mountains of paperwork and really did need to finish it before tomorrow. "Listen, if you don't have time, we can take a rain check."

"No, it'll be okay. I'm grateful that you agreed to be part of this."

Oh, great. Now she was joining him out of a sense of obligation. "I'm happy to do it. Please don't feel you have to keep me company while I eat. We can talk in the morning."

"No, let's do it now." She gave him a quick smile. "I'll lock up and be over there in a jiffy."

She clearly didn't want him hanging around while she took care of that. "See you there, then." He touched the brim of his hat.

Damned if that gesture didn't light up those amazing eyes of hers. Not for long, but this time he knew he wasn't mistaken. She was attracted to him. But for some unknown reason, she didn't want to be.

2

ONCE GRADY LEFT, Sapphire leaned against the nearest wall and groaned. How the hell was she supposed to get through tonight, let alone all the days and nights to follow, without jumping his bones? She'd hoped at least one of the co-op members would show up, but as much as they all wanted to meet Grady, every blessed person had other things going on.

She'd have to deal with his high-octane sexiness all by herself. Her hope that he wasn't as gorgeous as she'd remembered from their meeting three weeks ago had died the minute he'd appeared beside the barn. He possessed a lethal combo of cowboy charm, good looks and creative talent that spelled trouble in neon lights. He was her particular brand of kryptonite and she'd agreed to have dinner with him.

Refusing would have been rude, even though he'd given her a way out. He'd put his own work on hold and driven up here because she'd asked him to support the charity event. Although he was staying with Ben and Molly Radcliffe, he apparently wasn't expected there for dinner—another piece of bad luck.

Or maybe he'd been vague about his arrival time

so he'd be free to ask her to dinner. They'd sparked off each other three weeks ago and self-preservation should have stopped her from asking him to headline the event. But her love for the kitties and gratitude to the shelter had overcome her misgivings.

She had no one to blame for this mess but herself and she'd do it all again considering how many guests and potential donations he'd pull in. She'd just have to exercise restraint whenever they were alone together and make it clear that she wasn't interested. If the little voice in her head suggested that this man would be different, she wouldn't listen.

She had a weakness for creative men. But after four failed relationships with artistic guys, she'd finally admitted that she didn't belong with that type no matter how much they intrigued her. Some fatal flaw always turned up and doomed what had started out as something wonderful and promising. She was through taking chances.

After locking up, she drove her purple truck over to Scruffy's, a bar known for good food and live country music. The smell of barbecue made her mouth water as she climbed out of her pickup, tucked her keys in the pocket of her skirt and started for the door. The parking lot was full, as always, so at least they'd have plenty of chaperones.

"Hey, there." Grady walked toward her from the other side of the lot.

"Hi." She paused, captured by the sheer beauty of him. Ignoring that for the next few days would be impossible. The waistband of his Wranglers sat easy on his lean hips and his yoked Western shirt emphasized the breadth of his shoulders. She imagined sliding her palms up the soft material and feeling his muscles bunch beneath her hands. His wavy brown hair, worn collar length, would feel like silk between her fingers.

His smile brought her attention to his mouth. She could write an essay on the sensual contours of those sculpted lips. Men like Grady had usually perfected the fine art of kissing. His lips would be like velvet as they—

"Ready to go in?"

Great. She'd been caught ogling. She cleared her throat. "I thought you'd already be inside."

"I waited for you."

"Thanks." She risked looking into his brown eyes and her heart began to pound. Even shadowed by the brim of his hat, his gaze was hot. When a man looked at her that way, he had more than dinner on his mind— but she should talk after the way she'd checked him out.

The evening was taking on a familiar pattern. First they'd share a cozy booth and enjoy a meal along with some beer, which would loosen her inhibitions. Scruffy's casual atmosphere made it a great place for shedding inhibitions, especially on the dance floor. She could hear the music from here and it got louder every time someone went in or came out. Grady would ask her to dance to a slow tune and they'd rub against each other until they were both ready to combust.

After that she'd suggest heading to the little house she rented with her sister, who was conveniently out of town. They'd spend most of the night having amazing sex and the game would be on. She'd vowed never to take that path again with an art-making man.

Accepting his dinner invitation had been a bad idea. Yet changing the plan now would be a delicate operation. She hoped the excuse she was about to give him would do the trick. "You know, I hate to do this, but on the drive over I continued to think about all the paper-work I have waiting at home. Dinner would be lovely, but I really need to take a rain check."

"I see." He nudged back his hat, which allowed the light from the building to illuminate his square-jawed perfection.

"I'm really sorry, Grady. Organizing the event put me behind." True enough, but he didn't seem to be buy-ing it.

He gestured toward a spot away from the entrance and out of the glare of the lights. "Let's step over there for a minute, where it's not so loud."

"All right." She followed him into the shadows.

He paused and faced her, thumbs hooked in his belt loops. Sexy stance. "Sapphire, I'm interested in you and I get the impression you're interested in me. But if there's another guy, just say so. These things happen."

"There isn't anyone." Not for lack of trying to find a nonartist whose company she enjoyed. She'd dated an insurance adjuster, a dentist and a systems engineer. She hadn't clicked with any of them.

"Then why not have dinner with me?" He moved a little closer as his gaze held hers and a smile brought her attention back to his tempting mouth. "You have to eat sometime."

"I know, but…let's be honest." She took a deep breath. "It's not just about dinner, is it?"

His eyebrows lifted. "You want dessert, too? I dunno, Sapphire. That might stretch my budget." His grin faded. "No, you're right. It's not just about dinner, but if you don't have a boyfriend, what's the problem? Am I wrong that you kind of like me?"

"You're not wrong." God, he was potent. Being near

him fried her brain cells right when she needed to be alert. "But it'd be better if we just leave it at that."

"Why?"

"What if it didn't work out? That could make this week very awkward."

He smiled and drew closer still. "If that's all you're worried about, there's no problem. It'll work out."

"You seem pretty sure of yourself." Too bad she found that hot as hell.

"Normally, I'm not, but this time I have my reasons. We've had chemistry from the minute we laid eyes on each other three weeks ago. I've seen the way you look at me."

Heat sluiced through her. "Sorry. I'll stop doing that."

"Please don't stop on my account. I look at you the same way. Finding you at the Art Barn that day was a revelation. From what I can tell, you've allowed your true self to shine through and that turns me on. You make the sexiest pottery I've ever seen."

She laughed because he was the first person to say it out loud. No one else had dared. "Thank you."

"No, thank *you*. Holding it is quite an experience. I picture the way your hands molded each piece and I—"

"Um, right." If she let him go on in this vein, they'd never make it back to her house. They'd end up doing it in the back of a pickup, either hers or his. She'd thought their mutual attraction would be manageable. She'd never been so wrong.

"Lady, you and I generate a lot of heat. You can head home to catch up on paperwork but that's not going to change anything."

"Maybe not." She shoved her hands in her pockets and clutched her keys as a reminder that she was leaving. Just because he thought her surrender was inevitable, didn't mean he was right. But she could feel that heat he was talking about melting her resistance. "I need to go." She started to turn away.

"Hang on for a second." He lightly touched her arm.

The contact sent fire through her veins. "What for?" She turned back to him and saw the intent before he spoke the words.

"A kiss."

"No, that would be—"

"Only fair. I've been imagining kissing you ever since I drove away three weeks ago. If you don't want to take it beyond that point, I'll abide by that decision." He smiled. "What's one little kiss?"

A mistake. "I guess that would be okay."

"Not a very romantic answer." He drew her into his arms and lowered his head. "But good enough."

The velvet caress of his mouth was every bit as spectacular as she'd imagined. If she stuck to her guns, this would never happen again, so it seemed criminal to waste a single second of kissing Grady Magee. She hugged him close as he worked his magic. She'd figured the man could kiss, but she hadn't known the half of it. He started slow, tormenting her with gentle touches that made her ache for more.

When he finally settled in, she opened to him greedily, desperately wanting the stroke of his tongue. Kissing him was exactly what she'd been trying to avoid, but when he cupped her bottom and drew her against the hard ridge of his cock, she forgot why she'd been so reluctant.

Wouldn't a woman have to be crazy to reject this man? Wrapped in his strong arms and teased with his hot kisses, she craved the pleasure he promised.

Taking his mouth from hers, he continued to knead

her bottom with his strong fingers. "Still think we should nip this thing in the bud?"

Speaking of nipping…she wouldn't mind some of that, too. She gulped. "You've paralyzed my brain."

"Good." His mouth hovered over hers. "Maybe you think too much." And he delved deep again as he coaxed her to respond.

She didn't need much coaxing. With a low moan, she slid her arms around his neck and arched against his solid body. He answered with a low growl of pleasure and locked her in tight. She'd completely lost her mind.

In no time she'd thrust her tongue into his mouth. Somehow her hands moved from around his neck down to his firm butt cheeks. When his muscles flexed, she whimpered in frustration. There was only so much that could happen in the shadow of Scruffy's Bar and they'd reached the limit.

Breathing hard, he lifted his mouth a fraction from hers. "Okay, we're stopping now. But this isn't over."

She was incapable of speech, let alone an argument on that point.

Slowly he released her and backed away. "What time are you opening up tomorrow?"

She swallowed and frantically tried to remember. It finally came to her. "Seven."

"I'll be there. Take care, Sapphire." He touched the brim of his hat.

She turned and fled. If she didn't get out of there, she was liable to hurl herself back into his arms. Tomorrow she'd be stronger.

AFTER GRADY FINISHED his sandwich and beer at Scruffy's, he headed over to Ben and Molly's place. Although it seemed strange to be with them instead of at Thunder Mountain Ranch, they soon made him feel right at home. He had a chance to admire Ben's new saddle shop adjacent to the house and talk with Molly about her teaching job at Sheridan Community College and her curriculum planning for Thunder Mountain Academy. He also made friends with their golden Lab.

He found out from Ben and Molly that the charity benefiting from Sapphire's art event was the Fabulous Felines Cat Shelter. Fortunately, he was able to discuss the event and its organizer without letting his thoughts drift to that explosive kiss. But once he bid them goodnight and stretched out on their comfy guest bed, he could think of nothing else. Holding her had been even more perfect than he'd imagined.

They fit together as if designed for the passionate lovemaking she claimed they shouldn't have. Her soft breasts, her perfectly rounded ass and her supple lips taunted him relentlessly as he lay aroused and sweaty in the Radcliffes' guest room.

Maybe she really believed that getting involved would compromise their working relationship this week, but he hoped to change her mind. He fell asleep thinking of all the ways he could do that. Kissing would be a major part of the plan.

The next morning he dressed in his old scuffed boots, well-worn jeans and a faded chambray shirt. Leaving the black dress hat on the dresser, he picked up his everyday brown Stetson and left the Radcliffes' house after politely declining breakfast. They'd offered to fix him some, but that would have made him late.

He figured she'd be feeding the cats at seven. Ben and Molly had called it a feral cat colony. Although he wasn't familiar with the term, he could figure it out. The cats living in the woods weren't completely civilized, but they weren't completely antisocial, either. He could relate to that. There were times he longed to retreat into his studio and never come out. Other times he craved human companionship.

He wondered if other artists felt the same. This week would be a great time to find out if he was crazy or not. He was very different from his brother, a guide for white-water rafting trips. Liam was extremely social and even after all these years didn't totally understand Grady's need for solitude.

Dew sparkled on the grass when he pulled into the Art Barn parking lot a good thirty minutes early. Sapphire's purple truck wasn't there, so he sat with the windows rolled down and waited. The air smelled great and he wondered how often these days he took the time to simply *be*.

The sudden fame had taken him by surprise. Within a year he'd gone from living a somewhat solitary life in Alaska to being the darling of the Western art world. He was a beer-and-barbecue guy thrown into a champagne-and-caviar crowd and he still didn't quite have his footing. Being in Sheridan for this fund-raiser offered him the small-town ambiance he liked, maybe even needed.

Sapphire drove in and his body tightened. He couldn't remember ever wanting a woman this much. Maybe her reluctance to become involved with him played a part in that—the old forbidden-fruit ploy.

Because she didn't know him that well yet, she might be worried that he'd take off if the two of them had a spat. Raising money for the shelter was very important to her and she wouldn't want to jeopardize that. He wasn't sure how to convince her that he wasn't the kind of selfish SOB who would ruin her cherished event because they weren't getting along. Besides, they would get along. Oh, yeah, they certainly would.

Grabbing his water jug for later, he left his truck and closed the door with a minimum of noise. This time of the morning, traffic was light on the road that ran past the Art Barn, so birds chirping and warbling provided the only soundtrack. He liked sharing this peaceful setting with her.

Yet when he joined her as they walked to the front door, he could tell she was nervous. She gave him a quick smile and a breathy "Hi," but her hand quivered as she tried to open the door. Today she'd worn embroidered jeans and a tie-dyed blouse. Her colorful glass earrings reached to her shoulders and they tinkled as she worked with the key.

"Let me." He took the keys and got the door open. He fought the urge to cup her earrings in one hand to quiet the music while he nibbled on her tender earlobe. He'd read somewhere that earrings were a sexual invitation and he was more than ready to accept.

"Thanks. I must have had too much caffeine."

He hadn't had a drop but he was as wired as if he'd mainlined a whole pot. "Speaking of that, if you'll show me the coffee routine, I'll make some."

"I'll put some on. I'm sure you want to start setting up your equipment." Her gaze met his and skittered away.

"How about if I help you feed the cats first?"

"You don't have to." She gave him another quick glance, this one more pointed, as if silently warning him to back off.

"Are you worried that I'll scare Fred?"

She opened her mouth and then closed it again. Her

tiny sigh of resignation was almost too faint to hear. "If you come out with me and keep still, it should be fine."

"I can do that." He wasn't about to stay away from her, even though that was clearly what she thought she wanted. "Since they're the reason I'm here, I'd like to get better acquainted."

Her smile said she didn't quite believe that, but she nodded. "You can make the coffee while I fill the food bowls."

"Sounds like a plan." He followed her into the small space. Close quarters, which made it a great spot for a seduction, but he wasn't going to attempt one. He could feel the tension radiating from her. If he remained patient, she might surrender to it and seduce him, instead. Not this morning, but maybe before the week was over.

"The coffeepot and coffee are down there at the end. It's a basic model."

"Good. I like basic." He filled his water jug before making the coffee. He'd need the hydration once he started welding. "Ben and Molly said to say hi."

"They're good people." She got out the bowls and opened a bin of fishy-smelling dry cat food.

"They think the same of you. They're excited about this event to generate donations for the shelter."

She smiled at him. "Glad to hear it." She began scooping food into the bowls.

"Did you get your paperwork finished?"

"What paperwork?"

"You know, the paperwork you rushed home to work on last night."

"Oh…yeah." Her cheeks turned pink. "I didn't finish but I made a sizable dent in it. Thanks for asking."

He started the coffee perking and turned to watch her. "Actually, I didn't know until last night that the event is to raise money for the cat shelter and the work they do with feral colonies. Ben and Molly filled me in."

"I didn't tell you?"

"You might have. I wasn't focused on that aspect."

She paused and looked over at him. "Are you saying you only agreed to be here because of me?"

"Yes, ma'am." She might as well know it.

She groaned. "I didn't mean to give you the wrong idea."

"Or maybe you gave me the right idea. Three weeks ago I glanced in the rearview mirror as I was driving away from here and you were standing there watching me go. I extrapolated from that and figured we might have a good time when I came back." He held her gaze. "I still believe we can."

Her breath caught and desire shimmered in her turquoise eyes. He'd bet good money that if he tried kissing her again, she'd let him. They weren't in a public parking lot anymore, either. He imagined lifting her to the counter and unbuttoning her blouse.

The image was followed by thoughts of openmouthed kisses and intimate caresses as he sought the moist recesses of her trembling body. By the time he was finished loving her, they'd have bowls and cat food scattered everywhere and a mess to clean up. The cats still wouldn't be fed.

He took a calming breath. "We need to feed those cats."

3

SAPPHIRE COULDN'T DECIDE whether she was relieved or disappointed that Grady had passed up the chance to kiss her. Her thoughts had run in circles all night long, but one intriguing concept kept coming back around. What if they could have sex without any emotional entanglement?

The idea had merit. He lived in Cody, after all, and he was a very busy guy. She'd made the mistake of becoming emotionally invested in those other men and that had seemed to bring out the worst in them. If she didn't allow that to happen with Grady... Yeah, getting involved with him would still be somewhat of a risk, but he could be worth it.

She was touched that he'd wanted to interact with the cats this morning and that he'd taken it seriously enough to give the job priority. He'd clearly had other things on his mind a moment ago. Yet here he was helping her carry bowls out to the same spot where he'd found her the night before.

He glanced at her as they set the bowls in the grass. "Couldn't you just use a couple of large bowls?"

"I could, but some cats might be crowded out and not

get their fair share. This way I know everybody gets a decent helping."

"Must be tricky hauling them all out here by yourself."

"A little. I've learned to manage it."

He crouched down beside her, which meant she was able to breathe in the scent of his aftershave. Whatever he used had a smoky, seductive quality that suggested an activity involving hot bodies and soft sheets. Rolling around in the grass sounded like a good alternative. Being with Grady was a party waiting to happen.

If she didn't concentrate on something else, she'd be fighting the urge to grab him the entire time they were out here. "Normally, some of the cats would be here waiting but we're a little earlier than usual."

"So you're feeding them, but how does the shelter come into the picture?"

"The biggest contribution is medical." She kept her attention on the tree line as she looked for cats emerging from the shadows. "If we can get the cats into carriers, that's great, but mostly we have to trap them. Then they're either spayed or neutered, vaccinated and checked for any other issues. If the vet finds anything else, she treats it for the cost of the meds and supplies."

"Sounds like a great program."

"It is. The cats stay healthy but they don't keep adding more strays to the population."

"Have you figured out how the cats wound up here?"

She appreciated his interest. Questions about a topic dear to her heart made for a welcome distraction. "The first generation might have been barn cats when horses were housed in the stalls. Then the property was sold and the grain and the hay disappeared. Once the mice left, the cats had nothing to eat, so they likely moved to the woods and foraged for small rodents."

"And essentially became wild."

"They did." As she talked about the cats, her tension gradually eased. "But most of them seem to have retained a connection to people and to this barn. Fred's the least trusting. He joined the colony late and I don't think he liked being trapped and neutered."

"Do you blame him?"

She smiled at his look of horror. "We can't let them procreate."

"I get that and I'm all for population control. I just avoid thinking about the process."

"Are you squeamish?"

"Only when we're talking about cutting off—"

"Look." She pointed toward the trees. "Here they come."

"Where?" Squinting, he scanned the area.

"Over there, moving past the trunk of that big pine. Snow White's in the lead, as always. Grumpy, Sneezy and Dopey are following her." The little white female was always easy to spot, while the dappled shade camouflaged the others until they stepped out into the open.

"Okay, I see them."

"We're fairly sure those gray tabbies are Snow White's kittens because of the way she mothers them. And here comes Athena with her brood. They all got her butterscotch coloring except Persephone, the tortoiseshell. There's Fred, bringing up the rear."

"He sure does stand out."

"Yep. He was the hardest to catch. We finally got him in the trap using tuna as bait. I think the others would eat any flavor I put out, but I buy the fish kind because that's all Fred will eat."

"You're partial to him."

"I am. He's the smartest one and a survivor. He has several scars from the fights he's been in, but he beat the odds." She glanced at the approaching cats. "They seem a little uneasy about you being here. Maybe we shouldn't talk."

As they both fell silent, every cat settled down to eat except Fred, who stayed about six feet away with his green eyes fixed on Grady. Sapphire waited in hopes the cat would come forward on his own, but at last she decided he needed to be coaxed.

"Stay very still," she said, "while I try to sweet-talk him into coming over."

Grady gave a slight nod.

Leaning forward, she began crooning to the cat. "Come on, sweet Freddie. This man isn't going to hurt you." She lowered her voice. "Freddie, Freddie, Freddie. You know you want some. Come on, kitty-cat. That's a good boy."

Fred crept up to the bowl and began to eat, his teeth crunching on the small pellets. But that wasn't the only sound Sapphire heard. The rhythm of Grady's breathing had changed. She knew that rhythm because she'd heard it last night after he'd kissed her senseless.

She couldn't imagine why he was reacting that way, unless… She had to smile as she thought of a possible reason. She'd probably sounded damned seductive just now when she'd lured Fred up to the food bowl. Having a man around who was that susceptible to her was flattering. And arousing.

The cats made short work of the food. When it was gone, some moved away from the bowls and began grooming themselves. Snow White and Persephone came over for some head scratches, but Fred grabbed up one last bite before turning and scampering back to the woods as if he couldn't wait to leave.

"I'm determined to pet him someday."

"You probably will." Grady's breathing was back to normal.

"I think I will, too, eventually." She gave Athena some attention before she began gathering up the bowls. "Show's over for this morning, though."

He picked up the rest of the bowls. "I'll help you wash these."

"That's above and beyond. I know you want to get your area set up." She didn't feel ready to share the small space with him again. Besides, one of the other co-op members could show up at any moment and she didn't want to take a chance on major embarrassment. "I'll do it."

He must have heard something in her voice, because he didn't insist. "Thanks for letting me come along for the feeding routine."

"You're welcome. Did you pick any favorites?"

"Either Snow White or Athena. I haven't decided which."

"The two mama kitties."

"Yep." He held the door for her and followed her into the tiny kitchen. "I'm a real fan of mothers who stick by their kids. Like my mom did."

She put down the bowls and turned to him in surprise. "But you ended up in foster care at Thunder Mountain Ranch."

"And consequently, people think she abandoned us. Instead she was in a car accident and Rosie offered to take Liam and me until Mom was on her feet. Once she was okay, we went straight back to her. She's terrific."

"Does she live here?"

"Not anymore. She's in Cody with her new husband. Liam moved there when he got the job with the rafting company. I'd left to work in Alaska, so Liam talked Mom into moving down there with him. She met John in Cody. It all worked out."

"I can see that." Her heart squeezed as she thought of how tough those years when his mom was laid up must have been. "I'm glad for you. When we were in high school, all I knew was that you and your brother were at Thunder Mountain. I figured the two of you had no parents, or at least none that were worth anything."

He grimaced. "That's the only bad thing about going there. People assume we were neglected. Rosie's tried to set the record straight, but it's not easy. Thunder Mountain boys are supposed to be hard-luck cases."

"And some of them are."

"Yeah, just not me and Liam." He walked over to the coffeepot. "I'll get a cup of coffee and move out of your way."

"Will you start work on the sculpture for the event?"

"No, I'm saving that for the actual night." He took a mug out of the cupboard and poured coffee into it. "But I need to get comfortable with the space. Liam said Rosie would love to have one of my pieces, so that's what I'm going to make first to test the setup."

"That's so sweet!"

"I'm a sweet guy." He grinned. "So if you need me, I'll be in the back of the barn getting hot and sweaty." He picked up his coffee and left the kitchen.

Once he was gone, she took a deep breath before turning her focus to the bowls. She'd never washed those bowls so thoroughly. She scrubbed each one until her fingertips wrinkled while she tried to blot out the image of Grady's smile and his "getting hot and sweaty" comment. He wasn't going to let up on her.

Well, who could blame him? Last night she'd practically shrink-wrapped herself to his body. She'd barely escaped from the parking lot without begging him to come home with her.

She'd vowed on her way here this morning that this would be a new day and she'd keep her cool. That had lasted until he'd climbed out of his truck in his work clothes. He shouldn't have been as sexy in those as when he'd been dressed to impress, but apparently, it didn't matter what that cowboy wore. He had only to show up and she'd respond with a rapid pulse and damp panties.

Her lusty thoughts persisted even though he'd walked to the back of the barn at least fifteen minutes ago. The clank of metal and the hiss of a torch indicated he was working while she stood staring into space and wasting time.

Before his arrival yesterday she'd thought having him in the adjoining stall would be harmless fun, a chance to prove she could flirt without getting involved. Instead it looked as if she'd battle constant temptation with no relief in sight. She'd underestimated her sex drive, as well as his.

Swearing off artists had seemed like a piece of cake when she'd been smarting from the last humiliating breakup. Then Grady Magee had walked into her life. If the gods were testing her, they couldn't have given her a bigger challenge. He was better looking, sexier and more talented than any of the other four.

She had plans for today, though, and her wheel was waiting. Maybe once she immersed herself in the project, she'd forget that Grady was on the other side of the wall getting hot and sweaty. Yeah, right. Molding slick clay on a revolving wheel was a sensuous experience that would only make the situation worse.

One of the other co-op members was bound to come in shortly. She took courage from that as she walked down the aisle between the stalls. If she went straight into her work area without stopping by his, she might be okay.

The hissing of the torch stopped. "Is that you, Sapphire?"

"It's me."

"Could you give me some advice on this thing I'm making for Rosie?"

She could hardly refuse such a request. "Sure." Besides being flattered that he'd ask her opinion, she was curious about the design. He hadn't mentioned what he'd planned to create for his foster mother.

She felt the heat before she stepped inside the stall. He hadn't been kidding about the "hot and sweaty" part. His goggles hung around his neck and moisture had collected in the hollow of his throat. She wanted to dip her tongue into that depression and savor the salty taste.

Or maybe she'd comb his damp hair away from his forehead and unbutton the shirt that clung to his muscular chest. Booted feet braced apart and leather gloves tucked under one arm, he studied a sketch he'd tacked to the wall that separated his stall from hers. He'd laid an assortment of metal pieces on the floor beneath it.

She stifled a groan of frustration. Knowing he was the man who'd created the sculptures she'd seen in galleries had certainly made him appealing. Yet that was nothing compared to being in the same physical environment where he labored over his art. A visceral tug of longing almost made her reach for him. She clenched both hands and fought the impulse.

Something told her he wouldn't welcome a sexual advance right now, in spite of all the discussion they'd had on the subject. When he looked at her, his direct gaze was all business. He was in work mode. "This won't take long, I promise. I know you have your own stuff to do."

"No problem." His change of mood might have insulted another woman, but not her. She understood it. He'd entered his creative zone and had channeled all his sexual energy there. As long as he was focused on sculpting, she wouldn't have to worry about this attraction between them. She hadn't counted on that, because it was a rare gift, but one she respected. It also might explain why Grady had achieved such a high level of success.

"I thought I knew what I wanted when I sketched this," he said, "but now I'm rethinking the configuration. It's wolves."

"I can see that. Nice." The sketch was more than nice. He'd captured maternal love so perfectly that she had no doubt it was a mother with her litter.

"I picked a female wolf for Rosie because wolves have several pups. I'll make a bear for my mom because bears only have two."

Talk about irresistible. Now he'd added a layer of tender consideration to his blatant sexuality. "I'm sure they'll both be thrilled. The concepts are brilliant."

"I don't know about the brilliant part, but they're logical."

Oh, and FYI, the guy was modest. His admirable traits kept stacking up. "Trust me, both ladies will think the pieces are brilliant."

He laughed. "They do have an embarrassing tendency to gush. Okay, back to these wolves. My sketch has six pups but I think five is plenty. Maybe I should drop it back to four."

"Hmm." She studied his drawing. He'd arranged the wolves so they were all interconnected and would form a cohesive sculpture. She loved the symmetry of it.

"On a practical note, I'm one short of the recycled pieces I need for the pups' noses. I'd have to go looking for another one if I keep six, but dropping just one doesn't feel right for the composition."

"I'd leave them all in. You've already figured out how to do it, so taking one out means redoing the whole arrangement."

"But what about the nose thing? I don't know the scrapyards around here the way I do the ones in Cody."

"Could you alter one of the poses so the pup has his paw over his nose?"

"Maybe." He stepped toward the drawing. "That one. I could move the paw up without compromising the design." He turned to her with a smile. "Great idea. Thanks."

"You're welcome."

"Yeah, that'll work. Great suggestion." He repositioned his goggles, picked up his torch and grabbed one of the pieces of metal from the grouping on the floor. He acted as if he'd forgotten she was there.

Fascinating. She'd imagined having to fight off his advances, but it seemed that when he was working, he wouldn't be making any. That alone separated him from the other artists she'd dated. All of them, she realized now, had been easily distracted and basically lazy. They'd expected success to come to them without a whole lot of effort. They'd had ability and she'd allowed herself to be impressed with that, but ability without discipline was useless.

But comparisons to her ex-boyfriends didn't matter, because if she did decide to have sex with Grady, that was all it would be about. She'd keep it pure so she'd never have to discover his fatal flaw and become disillusioned for the fifth time. Could she manage to enjoy the sex and keep her emotions out of it? Only one way to find out.

Walking into her cubicle, she stared at her potter's wheel. She already had a plan for her next project, a large bowl to hold fruit. The interior would be a cool lime green and the exterior would be pale orange. She might add some flecks of yellow if she settled on the right shade.

Yesterday she'd been excited about making it, but today her thoughts were on Grady instead of the new piece that had been on the drawing board for more than a week. Several customers had said they'd buy such a bowl, so she'd already presold a few. On the other side of the wall Grady's torch hissed, and the air was filled with the acrid scent of hot metal.

Listening to those sounds galvanized her. She'd make that bowl this morning and have a prototype for the others. Each one would be slightly different because that was her hallmark, but she had to create the first one in order to make variations on that theme.

Generally, she preferred working alone in the barn, but having Grady there intent on his sculpting kept her at the wheel longer than she'd intended. His energy seemed to penetrate the barrier between them and she experienced design breakthroughs that stunned her. The fruit bowl took on an unusual shape that dipped on one side to leave room for a cascade of grapes or a cluster of bananas. She could see that becoming a trademark of her fruit-bowl designs.

She'd transferred the first one to the kiln and stopped by the kitchen to get coffee when Arlene Danbury came through the door. Arlene's watercolors of Wyoming landscapes had become increasingly popular in the past year, but the income wasn't enough for her to live on. She worked part-time as a nail tech in a local salon to make ends meet. She reminded Sapphire of a sparrow— always in motion and easily flustered.

This morning she was more hyper than usual. "He's here, isn't he? I can smell hot metal."

Sapphire felt like the gatekeeper, but if not her, then who? "He's working and I've learned he's very focused. We probably shouldn't disturb him."

"I wouldn't dream of it. But he'll take a break sometime, right? What's he working on? Is it the piece for the silent auction? I thought we were supposed to—"

"It's not for the silent auction." Sapphire had learned it was best to interrupt Arlene when she launched a barrage of chatter or it would go on forever. "He's making a sculpture for his foster mom. You know Rosie Padgett, right?"

"She's my client! I just did her nails this week. She'll be so thrilled. Is it a surprise? I'll bet it's a surprise, so I won't say anything. But if it's not a surprise, then she might think it's odd that I don't—"

"I think it's somewhat of a surprise but I didn't find that out. We'll ask him when he comes up for air."

"Okay. Let me get some coffee before I go back to my stall." She kept talking as she walked over to the pot. "I shouldn't have any more, because I'm already a little jumpy, but I work so much better when I'm sipping coffee. Wait, there's only enough for one cup. Did you want that?"

"Go ahead. I'll make more."

"If I'm the one to take the last of it, I'll make another pot. That's the way it always worked in my family. Maybe Grady wants some. Is he a coffee drinker?"

"I am." Grady appeared in the doorway to the kitchen. "But I can make it." Stepping through the door, he held out his hand. "Grady Magee, ma'am. Pleased to meet you."

For the first time in Sapphire's memory, Arlene was speechless. She stared up at the tall cowboy with her eyes wide and her mouth hanging open. After what felt like a very long time, she murmured, "You're beautiful." Then she pressed her hands to her pink cheeks. "Did I just say that out loud?"

Grady smiled. "If you think I look good, you should see my brother, Liam. He's the handsome one in the family."

"Then your mom and dad must be beautiful, too."

"Never knew my dad, but my mom is definitely beautiful." His gaze flicked over to meet Sapphire's as if to ask, *Who is this nutty lady?*

Since Arlene didn't seem aware that she'd failed to introduce herself, Sapphire decided she'd better do the honors. "Grady, this is Arlene Danbury. Her watercolors of the Bighorn Mountains are becoming quite popular."

Arlene's blush deepened. "Not as popular as your sculptures, Grady."

"They will be. I noticed your watercolors. Really nice."

"Oh, thank you! Pick whichever one you want and it's yours!"

He smiled at her. "You know I can't do that. I'd choose the best one and you'd be out a lot of money."

"I don't care."

"But I do. I'll buy one of your watercolors and be

honored to have the opportunity. Now, how about if I dump out the dregs and make us all a fresh pot of coffee?"

"Okay." Still dazed, Arlene nodded and moved out of his way. Then she turned to Sapphire and mouthed, *Oh, my God.*

Sapphire struggled not to lose it. At least she wasn't the only one enthralled with Grady. Arlene gradually recovered her poise and began pelting him with questions about his work. Surprisingly, she gave him a chance to answer each one before she threw out another, but it was more like an interview than a conversation.

He took it in stride, as if this happened to him quite a bit. Sapphire didn't doubt it. She couldn't recall his being followed by a pack of female admirers back in high school, but he'd filled out since then. And he'd taken up sculpting.

She'd bet his career choice affected how women perceived him. It certainly had influenced her. In high school he'd been a cute cowboy like all the others who attended school there. He still had cowboy charisma going on but he'd added a layer of intrigue with his career in the arts. No wonder Arlene had been struck mute.

But Sapphire had picked up another tidbit thanks to Arlene's fan-girl moment. He hadn't known his dad. In talking about his mother and Rosie, he'd skipped over any mention of his father. He'd quickly dismissed the subject just now, too. Come to think of it, Grady and Liam wouldn't have lived at Thunder Mountain Ranch if their father had been around to help out.

In a way she wished she hadn't learned that. It made him more vulnerable, more human and endearing. Because he hadn't elaborated, she didn't think the story

was a pretty one. He admired his mother because she'd
stuck by her kids and had raised them by herself, apparently, until the car accident had left her with no-
where to turn. That meant grandparents hadn't been
on hand, either.

Yeah, she really didn't want to know that about him.
Staying emotionally detached from a guy who looked
like Grady and had the talent of an angel was difficult
enough without finding out that he was fatherless, too.
Herb Padgett, Rosie's husband, would have taken that
role to some extent and maybe Grady's new stepdad had
belatedly become a father figure. But during Grady's
early years he'd missed out on having a dad for games
of catch or afternoons spent at the nearest fishing hole.

"Coffee's ready. Who wants a cup?" Grady held up
the pot.

"Me, please." Arlene stuck out her mug. "Thank you
so much for making it. Have you ever heated water for
coffee with a welding torch? I knew a guy who used to
do that all the time, made me so nervous. I told him a
million times not to do it but he thought it was a cool
idea. In my opinion—"

"Fortunately, I don't do that." Grady held up the pot.
"Sapphire? Coffee?"

"Sure. Thanks."

He poured it and tossed her a wink when Arlene
started in on unsafe-welding-torch stories again. "If
you ladies will excuse me, I'm gonna take my coffee
and get back to work."

"Me, too," Arlene said. "I'll walk you down there."

"That would be great." Grady gave Sapphire a quick
smile before leaving with Arlene.

Her voice drifted back as they started down the barn
aisle. "Can I peek in on your project?"

"Not yet, ma'am." Grady sounded polite but firm. "If you don't mind, this is a very personal sculpture, so I'd like to make a lot more progress before I show it to anyone."

"Oh, sure, sure. I totally understand." Arlene must have realized she was being pushy. "I'll just stop off here at my stall, then. See you later!"

Nicely handled, Sapphire thought. Knowing he'd trusted her enough to seek her advice about the piece created a warm glow that she carried with her as she returned to her wheel. But her plan to keep her emotional distance wasn't working worth a damn. That could be a problem.

4

BY THE END of the day Grady had met five of the co-op members and made good progress on Rosie's sculpture. He needed another two days to finish it so he could take it to the ranch when he went there for supper. He'd sworn the other artists to secrecy and everyone had agreed to warn him if by some chance Rosie stopped in at the Art Barn.

He didn't think she would. The last week of classes for Thunder Mountain Academy was always a busy time and she'd be needed out there. His surprise should stay safe until he presented it to her. He'd get Cade to help him set it up while Rosie was busy in the kitchen. They could always move it later if she wanted it in a different spot.

Right now, though, he knew it must be about time to feed those cats and he wanted to help. Working all day had felt good and he wasn't as desperate to make something happen with Sapphire as he had been when he'd first arrived. Or so he thought until he walked into the kitchen.

She had the phone to her ear and her back to him as she pulled bowls out of the cupboard. His timing had been excellent for watching her unobserved. He paused to admire how her embroidered jeans hugged her ass. His palms itched to feel her muscles flex the way he had last night in the shadows at Scruffy's.

That remembered sensation triggered a replay of others—the warmth of her lush body, the heat of her mouth and the sound of her moans. They'd been so damned close to making the leap. He didn't want to get that close again unless he felt fairly certain they'd go the distance.

He'd outgrown the teasing phase of a sexual relationship a long time ago. Yeah, a certain amount of dancing around was fun, but eventually, he liked to know where he stood. With Sapphire he still wasn't sure. She was giving him mixed signals.

"I'm glad the gig's working out for you, sis." She opened the bin and reached for the scoop.

He rapped on the doorframe so he wouldn't scare her. When she turned, he entered the kitchen and took the scoop out of her hand. Then he waved her off and began dishing food into the bowls so she could finish her conversation.

"The event is looking good." She leaned against the counter and watched him work. "Having Grady Magee on board doesn't hurt." She listened for a moment. "There is? What's it of?" She held eye contact with him. "That sounds really cool. I'll tell him how much you like it. I'd better go. Time to feed the kitties. Love you!" She disconnected. "Thanks for doing that."

"I figured it was about time for the evening meal."

"You figured right." She put the phone on the counter. "That was my sister, Amethyst. Do you remember her?"

"Sure. She had the lead in the school musical one

year." Amethyst had been the flashier of the two. Plenty of guys had lusted after Sapphire's younger sister, especially after she'd belted out "Santa Baby" during a Christmas choral program.

Sapphire laughed. "Everybody remembers Amethyst. You didn't ever date her, did you? She went out with so many guys that I lost track."

"No, we didn't date." Thank God. He and Sapphire had enough obstacles without adding the weirdness of having dated her sister. "What's she up to these days?"

"Professional singer. She followed my dad's musical lead."

"Does he still have that jazz band?"

"The members have shifted around and the name's changed a couple of times, but yep—he loves it."

"That's cool. And your mom's still teaching art?"

"Absolutely. I asked her to be part of this co-op but she really doesn't have time. Maybe when she retires."

He enjoyed watching the love shine in her eyes as she talked. "Creative family you have there."

"Yeah, I feel lucky. Anyway, Amethyst mentioned that one of your sculptures is in the lobby of the Jackson Hole resort where she's performing for the next two weeks."

"I have a couple over there. Which one?"

"It's the waterfall fountain that goes into a pool at the bottom with a doe and buck drinking. She said it's huge."

"Twenty-two feet eight inches, to be exact."

"Wow."

He filled the last bowl and closed the bin. "I took it up there in sections and finished the welding on the spot."

"That must have caused quite a stir among the resort guests."

"It did. I offered to complete it in the middle of the night but the management thought it would be more dramatic if people could see the final construction phase. It was great PR but I'd still rather work in the privacy of my studio."

"Is our evening event going to be a problem for you?"

He gazed at her. "It's not my favorite way to create, but like I said last night, I wasn't concerned about the how. Only the who."

"I know." Her quick swallow betrayed her uneasiness.

"Forget I said that."

She gave him a rueful glance. "Not likely. But right now it's feeding time. We've tried to keep a regular schedule they can count on. It's part of building trust."

"Makes sense." He pondered that as he helped her carry out the bowls. Trust was an issue between them, too. Whether she didn't trust him or herself wasn't clear, but either way, she expected bad things to happen if they gave in to this attraction.

"You can put the bowls down now. They're waiting."

"Right." While he'd been lost in thought, she'd stood waiting as the cats milled around at their feet. "Sorry."

"It's just good to put all the bowls down together so they each have one."

"Makes sense. But Fred's not here. Do we wait for him?"

"No. He'll be along. Sometimes he hangs back."

"Okay." He lined up the ones he carried, dropped to his knees and sat back on his heels. "Sorry for holding up the show. I got distracted."

"I've noticed that doesn't happen when you're working on a sculpture. You're incredibly focused."

He couldn't resist the opening she'd given him. "That's one of two activities that get my undivided attention."

"And the other is football?"

Kidding around was a good sign they were making progress. "Guess again."

Her breathing quickened. "You're too sexy for your own good, Grady."

"Too sexy for you?" He glanced over at her.

"I didn't say that." She kept her attention on the tree line as she watched for Fred, but her cheeks had turned a pretty shade of pink.

His pulse hammered. Maybe he'd built up a little trust, after all. "Any chance I can cash in that rain check so we can have dinner tonight?"

"I think— Oh, my goodness. Who's that?"

A large gray cat left the shelter of the woods and bounded toward them.

"You don't recognize it?"

"Nope. And he's not acting like a feral."

"How can you tell it's a male?"

"I'm not positive but he looks like a tom to me."

The cat marched right up to the food bowl at the end of the row, within arm's reach of Grady, hunkered down and began to devour the food. When Fred showed up, the bowls were all occupied. He surveyed the line of cats before sitting down and fixing his green eyes on Grady as if he might be to blame for this fiasco.

"Stay here." Sapphire slowly rose to her feet. "I'll bring out another bowl for Fred."

"Good idea. He's giving me the stink eye."

As she backed away carefully, Fred stood, arched his

back and hissed. Then he retreated a few feet while the other cats continued to munch.

"She's going to get you food, bozo," Grady said. "Show some appreciation."

Fred sat down again and glared at him, but the gray cat looked up at the sound of Grady's voice.

Blinking, he studied Grady with eyes as blue as a midday sky. Then he went back to eating the last few nuggets in the bowl. Athena had taken the spot next to him and she still had food. He sidled over as if to grab some but she gave a warning growl and he retreated.

After searching his bowl for any crumbs, he gave up and stared at Grady some more. Then he made a noise low in his throat that was neither meow nor purr. Must have been a greeting of some kind, because he walked around the bowl and came over to rub against Grady's thigh.

"Hey, there." Grady gently scratched behind the cat's ears and was rewarded with a soft purr. "You're no feral, are you, buddy? You're somebody's pet." He noticed burrs and matted hair in what was otherwise a luxurious-looking coat. "Or were somebody's pet a while ago. What happened?"

In response, the cat tried to crawl into his lap. But Grady was kneeling, which meant the lap situation was never going to work out. Instead he scooped the cat into his arms. In midmotion he realized it could be a very dumb move. He didn't know this animal and he could decide to bite or scratch him.

That didn't happen. Purring even louder, the cat settled in and tucked his head under Grady's chin. Although his appearance suggested he'd be heavy, he was extremely light. All that hair disguised the fact that he was skin and bones.

"Wow, that's amazing."

Sapphire's murmured comment took Grady by surprise. He hadn't heard her come back, probably because he'd been involved with his new friend and she'd been moving as quietly as possible to avoid disturbing the cats as they finished their meal. He gazed at her over the top of the gray cat's head as he stroked its tangled fur. "What now?"

She set down the bowl for Fred, who came over with more enthusiasm than he'd shown the last two times. "We have to find out if someone's missing a cat. He obviously used to have a home."

"Yeah, but I don't think he's been there in a while. He's pretty thin."

"And his coat's a mess."

"But he's friendly as all get-out."

She smiled. "I noticed." She petted the butterscotch mama cat, who'd come over with her look-alike family. The others lounged in the grass, either grooming their coats or watching the interaction between Grady and the cat in his arms.

Fred finished his meal and moved away from the dish, but instead of leaving, he sat down and stared at Grady.

Sapphire watched the tuxedo cat. "That's a switch. He's never hung around after the meal before."

"Maybe he sees me loving up this one and thinks it looks like fun."

"I hope so. It would be great if I could hold him the way you're holding our newcomer." She sighed. "Not that I could take him home. My sister's allergic."

"You both still live at home?"

"No. By *home* I meant the little house we rent together. She's a perfect housemate except for the fact that I can't have a cat. She's offered to take meds so I can adopt one but I don't want to put her through that. Eventually, we'll each get a place and until then I can work with the shelter and the ferals. It's fine."

"How about having a barn cat?"

"We've all talked about it. Naturally, we'd want one of our ferals, but we can't split up the mamas and their kittens, which leaves Fred, and he's so not ready. Ah, there he goes." She stood. "Guess it's time to figure out a plan for this new guy."

"What are the options?" Grady levered himself to his feet and felt little pinpricks on his chest as the cat dug his claws into his shirt and held on.

"I should probably drive him over to the shelter. They can keep him for the night while we check around and see if anybody's reported losing a cat that fits his description."

Sensible as that sounded, Grady didn't want to do it. The cat seemed to have chosen him as a savior and he couldn't picture handing this skinny creature over into someone else's care, although the shelter staff was obviously capable.

"You're frowning. What's the matter?"

"I just… I want to keep him company until we find out what the story is."

"Oh." Her expression grew soft. "That's sweet."

"And impractical. I don't want to haul him over to Ben and Molly's. It's an imposition. We don't know anything about this cat, and besides, they have a dog who may or may not react well to cats."

"I agree you can't take him there." She gathered up the bowls. "Bring him into the barn and we'll figure something out."

"Hey, here's an idea. We probably shouldn't give him the run of the place, but I could make up a bedroll and stay with him in the office tonight." That plan screwed up his hope of having dinner with Sapphire, but he couldn't abandon this animal that had latched on to him, literally.

Cradling the gray tom, Grady followed Sapphire into the barn. Along the way he found himself talking to the cat and assuring him everything was going to be fine. It would be if Grady had anything to say about it. The members of the feral colony seemed satisfied with their life in the woods. But Gandalf wasn't suited for that.

Grady had named him without realizing it. Of course, someone had already given this cat a name but that person wasn't here to supply the info, so might as well come up with a new identity. Years ago Grady had seen *The Lord of the Rings* and he'd been fascinated with Gandalf the Grey. Gandalf's wand had seemed a little like a welding torch. Point it in a certain direction and stuff happened.

Sapphire led the way into the kitchen and dumped the bowls in the sink. "First I should check him for fleas."

"Gandalf doesn't have fleas."

Her azure eyes sparkled with amusement. "How do you know his name?"

"I don't, but we can't keep calling him *the gray cat*. I've decided his name is Gandalf."

"It's a good name. I watched those movies, too. But naming him Gandalf doesn't magically rid him of fleas or ear mites." She turned on the overhead light. "Hang on to him while I have a look."

Grady was treated to the sensual pleasure of holding a warm, purring cat while listening to Sapphire's sexy voice as she examined Gandalf for fleas. The combination had a predictable effect but he pushed those thoughts aside. The cat's welfare came first.

"We're in luck," she said. "He doesn't have fleas or ear mites. Did you happen to see if he'd been neutered?"

"Nope, didn't notice."

"Then shift him around so I can peek under his tail."

"Does it matter? It's not like we're going to arrange a hot date for him."

"It matters. If he's an unneutered male, he could decide to mark his territory and that smell is nasty. Just move your arm so I can check. Oh, good. Nothing's there."

Grady leaned down and put his mouth next to the cat's ear. "Don't be offended, buddy. I'm sure you had a nice pair while they lasted."

"Oh, for heaven's sake." Sapphire rolled her eyes.

"Never mind. It's a guy thing."

"I'm sure it is, but Gandalf's better off without his equipment. It would only have gotten him into trouble."

"That much I agree with."

Her laughter rippled through him, setting off little explosions of joy along the way. He wanted to spend more time laughing with her and less time discussing whether they should get it on. If she'd just loosen up and let things happen, she'd discover how nicely everything would work out.

Scratching behind Gandalf's ears, he turned to her. "Now that he's passed inspection, can I keep him with me tonight if I bed down in the barn?"

"That's one option."

"I'd rather do that than take him to the shelter. I'm sure they're great, but he's been separated from the people he counted on. He's pinned his hopes on me and I don't want to let him down."

"There's another option. I could take him home with me."

"What about your sister's allergies?"

"It should be okay if I confine him to my bathroom and scrub it down after he leaves. Now that I know he doesn't have any parasites and he's neutered, I'm willing to give it a shot."

Grady didn't have to think twice about it. "That's a generous offer, but I'd still rather keep him with me here in the barn. I have a couple of blankets in the truck. Gandalf and I will make out just fine."

"But there's no people food here except maybe a leftover sandwich in the fridge from someone's lunch."

"I have a phone and I know how to use it. I'll order pizza."

She smiled. "What a coincidence. I'm ordering pizza tonight, too."

"From Geppetto's?"

"Is there any other place?"

"Not in my opinion. I found out last time I was here that they're still in operation. During my Thunder Mountain days we'd all get together in one of the cabins after Rosie and Herb had gone to bed and order up food. Pizza, calzones, bread sticks and enough soda to float a battleship."

"My sister and I used to do that, too, especially if we'd organized a slumber party. We'd meet the delivery guy in the driveway so he wouldn't ring the doorbell."

"We didn't have to worry about that. We'd just direct him to come around by the back road. I wonder if Rosie and Herb knew all about it."

"I can't speak for them, but my folks certainly did. They told us later that they'd lie in bed laughing at the lengths we went to, as if they'd be upset because we ordered pizza. But doing it in stealth mode is part of the fun."

"I know. If I'd kept this pizza plan to myself, it could have been Gandalf's and my stealth pizza move."

"But since you didn't…" She paused as if weighing what she was about to say. "Want to share a pizza?"

"You want to stick around and eat pizza with Gandalf and me?" Okay, she had to trust him at least a little if she was willing to hang out alone with him at the barn for a while. He looked down at the cat in his arms. "What do you say, Gandalf?" He rubbed the cat under the chin. "Shall we invite the lady to a gourmet pizza dinner in the barn?"

Gandalf's purr ramped up a notch.

"I think that's a definite yes." He glanced at her. "What do you like on your pizza?"

Her eyes shone as if ordering a pizza was a really big deal. "Everything."

Maybe it was a big deal. If so, he was glad he'd brought it up. "Great. Me, too. You'll have to order it, though. Gandalf's sticking to me like Velcro."

"Okay." She picked up her phone from where she'd left it on the counter. "But unless you really want to sleep on a bedroll in the office tonight, I think we should have the pizza delivered to my house."

"Your…" He stared at her. "Are you sure?"

"Very sure." Reaching out, she stroked the cat and let her hand rest on his arm as she met his gaze. "Come home with me, Grady."

Somehow he got the words out. "I'd like that."

5

AFTER A DAY spent debating whether to risk a brief fling with Grady, Sapphire had rounded the side of the barn to find him cradling a stray cat. He couldn't have chosen a more seductive move. Ironically, the presence of the cat had kept her from throwing herself into his arms and begging him to take her right there in the grass.

So she'd had to table her lust until they'd decided what to do. Grady's protective behavior toward the cat complicated things, but once she'd decided Gandalf could stay in her bathroom, she'd hatched her plan. She'd had no trouble convincing Grady to cooperate, but he'd vetoed the cat carrier.

Consequently, they'd had to leave his truck at the Art Barn so he could hold Gandalf while she drove. The August evening was cool enough that they could leave the windows up and not have to bother with air-conditioning, but she hadn't anticipated that sharing a confined space with Grady would be such an erotic experience. Breathing in all that masculinity turned her into a juicy woman with sex on the brain. She could now testify that pheromones existed.

She was in charge of this operation, though, which

meant figuring out how to make Gandalf comfortable once they arrived at her house. Only then would she be able to satisfy her craving for the man holding the cat. She had a decorative basket at home and a plush throw that would make a soft bed. An old plastic storage tote would work as a temporary litter box. To increase the odds that Gandalf would stay in the bathroom without crying, she'd give him some tuna.

When they'd started this journey, the cat had clung to Grady and mewled, but Grady's murmured words and gentle stroking eventually worked. She couldn't hear what he was saying, but the soothing sound of his voice finally convinced Gandalf it was safe to unhook himself from Grady's shirt and curl up in his lap.

Probably a good thing on many levels. She'd been way too focused on Grady's lap ever since they'd left the Art Barn. Now it was blocked from view by a fluffy gray cat. But Gandalf had made little holes in Grady's shirt and probably in his skin, too, although he'd never once complained.

She didn't want to let that go untended. "You probably have some puncture wounds."

"It's okay. He didn't mean to."

"Of course not. But once we get him settled, you'll need to wash any scratches with soap and water. Then I'll give you some tea tree oil to put on them so they won't get infected."

He wrinkled his nose. "Nah. It smells funny."

"I've always kind of liked it."

"Oh, well, then." He chuckled. "Give me a gallon of the stuff."

"In moderation."

"How about you rub it on me so I get just the right amount?"

"How about we drop the subject before I run into a tree?"

He looked over at her. "Conversation getting a little hot for you?"

"Yes." The scent of virile male combined with the thought of rubbing oil on his bare chest had created a persistent throbbing between her damp thighs.

Grinning, he leaned back in his seat. "Good to know."

"We can't get carried away, though."

"I disagree. I intend to get completely carried away."

She swallowed a moan. "I meant not until—"

"I know. Just teasing you. But the good news is that Gandalf's about to doze off."

She glanced at the cat, whose eyes were at half-mast. "I'll go in first and get everything together. Then you can take him straight into the bathroom so he has no chance to bolt."

"Right. Maybe he won't even wake up."

"He'll wake up, probably when I stop the truck. Cats aren't like little kids. They can look sound asleep when they're only dozing. But I'm sure he's exhausted from trying to survive on his own. If I have his new spot all organized and add in a can of tuna, maybe he'll eat that and go back to sleep instead of crying for you."

"I talked to him about the crying thing."

"Oh, did you, now?"

"No, really, I did. He knows what's on the line. He won't bother us."

"Have you been around cats much?"

"Mostly the barn cats when I lived at Thunder Mountain. They were easy, liked everybody."

"Whereas Gandalf seems partial to you. If he isn't happy with the separation, he'll cry."

Grady shook his head. "Nope, not gonna happen. Gandalf and I have an agreement."

"What sort of agreement?"

"That's between us guys."

Damn, but he was adorable. "We're about to find out if you're right. This is my street. Oh, and once you're closed in the bathroom with him, you should take off your shirt."

"Hell, why stop there?"

"Slow down, cowboy. The shirt's to tuck into the basket I'm planning to use for his bed. Your shirt will smell like you and might comfort him so he won't cry."

He winced. "I'll bet it does smell like me, which is not a plus. I apologize for perfuming your cab with my sweaty body. My plasma torch gives off a lot of heat."

"No problem." If only he knew.

"In fact, I predict Gandalf will take one whiff of that shirt and refuse to set foot in the bed. Don't you have a nice cozy blanket, instead?"

"I'll use a blanket, too, but the shirt on top will make all the difference. Animals don't have the same hang-ups about body odor as people do. They love it." *And when it comes to you, so do I.*

"If you say so, but that brings up another point. The rest of me is pretty ripe, too. I could use a shower before we move on to the next stage."

Over her dead body. "But that would disturb Gandalf."

"Do you have another shower I could use?"

"My sister's bathroom is upstairs, but—"

"Would it be okay if I showered up there? I'll clean up after myself."

"We'll talk about it after we get Gandalf settled, okay?" She didn't plan to talk at all. She'd grab the tea tree oil and a box of condoms out of her cabinet while she was arranging everything. Grady could wash his scratches in the kitchen sink and if she had her way, he'd forget all about that shower he thought he needed.

She pulled into the driveway of the two-story Victorian. "I think it'll be less trouble if I don't park in the garage."

"Me, too." He tipped back his hat and peered out the windshield. "Cute house."

"It works for us. I took the master downstairs and Amethyst has the entire second floor. The landlady let her soundproof one of the bedrooms so she could have a small recording studio."

"Accommodating landlady."

"She's the best, which is one reason we aren't rushing to move." She turned off the engine and hoped Gandalf wouldn't wake up, but those blue eyes popped open immediately. Next thing she knew, he was fastened to Grady's chest again. "Just stay put for now. I'll get everything ready and come back for you."

"We'll be here." Grady wrapped the cat in his arms and started talking to him, although he kept his voice so low Sapphire couldn't discern the words. Maybe he was reminding Gandalf of their agreement.

"Be back as soon as I can." She climbed slowly out of the cab so she wouldn't startle the cat even more. "I'll close my door just in case."

"He's not going anywhere."

She didn't think so, either, but she shut her door anyway. A carrier would have made transportation easier, but it probably would have freaked out the cat. Despite Grady's assurances, she wondered if Gandalf would sit on the other side of the bathroom door and yowl once they closed him away from his hero. That would pretty much cancel out having sex.

She had to laugh as she hurried up the porch steps and across to the door. What if it turned out that a cat threw a monkey wrench into her plans? If that happened, she should probably take it as a warning that she was making a mistake. But if Gandalf didn't interfere, was that the universe blessing the idea of a fun romp with this appealing man?

She quickly arranged everything for Gandalf and was about to go back outside when she remembered the tea tree oil and the condoms. The lamp table beside her four-poster had no drawer. Rather than put the condoms on the table in the open, she shoved them under the bed skirt.

If Gandalf protested being closed in the bathroom, she didn't want a box of condoms in plain view taunting them with what they weren't doing. The tea tree oil, though, could go on top of the table. She planned to have a really good time doctoring Grady's wounds.

The light was fading from the sky as she walked around to the passenger side of her truck. "Okay in there?"

"You bet. Open 'er up."

She opened the door cautiously because she still had visions of Gandalf making a break for it. If she was right about his history, he'd been deceived by humans before and might decide freedom was his best option. But he stayed firmly attached as Grady eased out of the truck.

"Follow me." She led the way to the front porch. She and Amethyst had spent many nights in the white wicker rocking chairs drinking wine. It was during one of those nights that Sapphire had promised her sister that she'd never date an artist again.

This wasn't dating, though. She opened the door and let Grady go in first. Dating implied building something solid. They wouldn't build a damn thing other than memories of great sex.

"Go down the hall and turn right," she said. "That's the master bedroom. The bathroom's connected to it."

"This is a first for me. I've never walked into a woman's bedroom carrying a cat."

"Then we're both breaking new ground. I've never invited a man into my bedroom who was holding a cat."

"I guess you wouldn't, considering the allergy problem. I'll bet your bedroom doesn't usually smell like tuna, either."

"No, but Gandalf is very interested in that aroma."

Grady hoisted the cat a little higher on his shoulder. "I know. I can feel him quivering. Want something yummy, Gandalf?"

The cat meowed.

"Okay, then remember our deal. You get tuna and I get—" He paused to check out the bed. "Four-poster, huh?"

"I decided to buy something that fits the time period of the house."

"Hmm."

"What?"

"Oh, just thinking."

She caught an erotic undertone that shifted her pulse into high gear. "About what?"

"Never mind." He glanced at her. "We can have that discussion a little later. But I do need to ask you about one item we'll need. Do you have—"

"I do."

"Good. I was hoping." He walked into the bathroom

with Gandalf. "Go ahead and shut the door. I've got this."

After closing the door with as little noise as possible, she sat on the bed and waited while she tried not to think about what was supposed to happen next. It might or it might not, depending on Gandalf. Because of the uncertainty, she shouldn't count on anything.

She shivered in anticipation anyway. Although the low rumble of Grady's voice was muffled by the door, Gandalf's high-pitched meows came through clearly. A conversation was taking place.

She couldn't help smiling at the idea of this broad-shouldered cowboy communicating earnestly with a homeless cat. She didn't think Gandalf would stay homeless, though. Through her volunteer work with the shelter, she'd seen enough instances of bonding that she expected Grady would take the cat. Perhaps the family would be found, but none of the lost-cat pictures she'd seen taped to light and telephone poles around town had resembled Gandalf.

Negotiations continued on the other side of the bathroom door. Then the strip of light shining under the door went out. More soft murmurs followed, interspersed with cat noises that were a blend of purrs and meows. Finally, all was quiet.

Moments later the door opened and Grady stepped out, shirtless. She took a moment to absorb the lust-inducing sight of his muscled chest with its light dusting of brown hair. Oh, yeah. She'd made the right decision inviting him here.

He must have left his hat in the bathroom, too, because he was no longer wearing it. His hair looked tousled, as if he'd been running his fingers through it. "Gandalf will be fine. He loves the tuna." He seemed relaxed, but a second glance revealed that his eyes had darkened to the color of chocolate.

She picked up the small bottle of tea tree oil and stood. "Now we'll go into the kitchen and wash your puncture wounds."

He eliminated the distance between them. "What if I feel like kissing you first?"

When she placed a hand on his chest to keep him from doing that, the tactile pleasure of soft hair against her palm distracted her from her purpose. But then she noticed the little red dots tattooed on his warm skin by Gandalf. The wounds should be tended to right away.

Cupping her chin, he tilted her head up to meet his smoldering gaze. "The cat's settled in. I've been waiting to do this all day."

"Wait! We both know that once you kiss me, it'll be all over."

"All *over*?" He grabbed her hand and pressed it to his rapidly beating heart. "You insult me, lady. Yeah, I was a three-second wonder when I was seventeen, but I've learned a few things since then."

His heat traveled from her palm to her entire body, leaving her quivering and oh so ready to find out what he'd learned. "I didn't mean it that way."

He brought her hand to his lips and kissed the tips of her fingers. "That's a relief. I was afraid you'd talked to a couple of my old girlfriends. I didn't do right by them but I didn't know it at the time. Now they're married and have kids. I don't think it's appropriate to contact them and say, 'I'm so sorry that I didn't last long enough for you to come.'"

"Yeah, that's a bad idea." The brush of his lips over her fingers left her short of breath. "I doubt their husbands would appreciate it."

"For the record, I've developed a fair amount of stamina."

"I'm sure you have." God, how she wanted him, but she forced herself to be sensible. "Before you prove it to me, let's go in the kitchen and wash your puncture wounds."

"Not necessary. I'll shower in a minute. I just need to kiss you first."

"Humor me. I want to make sure we clean those scratches." Tugging on his hand, she pulled him toward the bedroom doorway. "I thought you were looking forward to having me rub your manly chest with tea tree oil."

"I've changed my mind. Now I have different locations where I want you to rub. After I get cleaned up, I'll point them out."

But he let her coax him into the vintage kitchen. Reconditioned antique appliances and lace curtains always made Sapphire feel as if she'd stepped back in time. Normally, she walked in here and had the urge to sip tea and do needlepoint.

Not tonight. "Stand right there." She let go of his hand. "I'll get soap and a dishcloth."

"I can see you're determined about this."

"I am."

He glanced around. "This house has character. I like it."

"Me, too." She liked it even better with him in it. Dampening a cloth, she squirted it with liquid soap, then walked back to him. "This'll just take a minute."

"Then I get my kiss?"

"Absolutely." She rubbed the cloth over his chest.

"Yikes, that's cold!"

"Sorry! Want me to wait for the water to warm up?"

"No, but give me that." He took the cloth, rubbed it briskly over his chest and tossed it on the counter. "Good enough." He pulled her into his arms.

"But you still have soap on you!"

"Don't care." He lowered his head.

"And we didn't put on the tea tree—" She didn't finish the sentence. His mouth came down on hers with an urgency that made her gasp.

With a low growl, he delved deep with his tongue. Moments later he grasped her bottom to tug her against his stiff cock while he ravished her mouth as if he couldn't get enough. She couldn't get enough of him, either. Holding his head, she kissed him back as frustration gave way to delicious passion.

He lifted his lips from hers for a second and gulped for air. "I could gobble you up." Then he shifted angles and urged her to open wider for the sensual thrust of his tongue.

She'd never been kissed with such energy and power. Lost in a whirlpool of sensation, she clung to him as her heartbeat thundered in her ears and moisture sluiced between her thighs. His grip tightened on her bottom. Without breaking the kiss, he lifted her to the counter, freed her blouse from the waistband of her jeans and began unbuttoning it.

Maybe he was a mind reader as well as a talented kisser, because her breasts ached for the sweet tug of his mouth. Reaching behind her, she unfastened her bra, and in seconds both items lay on the counter. Only then did he end the kiss and step back.

She reveled in his hungry expression as he gazed at her. Cradling a breast in each hand, she brushed her thumbs over the aroused nipples while she watched the fire blaze in his eyes.

"Magnificent," he murmured.

"Touch me."

"Oh, I intend to." Stepping forward, he cupped her hands as his gaze burned into hers. "I imagined doing this in the kitchen at the barn." He slowly drew her hands away. When he replaced them with his own, he closed his eyes and sighed. "Like silk."

Her heart pounded so fast she grew dizzy. "Only warmer."

"Much warmer." He opened his eyes and looked into hers as he began a slow massage. "When I saw your work, I knew…"

Her breath hitched. "Knew what?"

"That you'd be sexy as hell, ready for anything."

"*Oh*, yeah." She let out her breath. She'd been so afraid he'd say something about fate or kismet.

Instead he watched her eyes as he kneaded her breasts. "You're sensitive here."

"Mmm."

"I thought you would be." His breathing roughened. "Lean back."

Bracing her hands behind her, she tilted away from him and propped her head against the cabinet door.

Still holding her gaze, he unfastened her jeans and drew the zipper down. "Lift up." When she did, he deftly peeled her jeans over her hips and shoved them to her knees.

She trembled with need. "I thought this was only going to be a kiss."

"Ah, but I didn't say where I was going to kiss you. A guy would be crazy to limit himself when there's so much to enjoy." His glance traveled from her mouth to her breasts and finally to her moist panties. Then he returned his attention to her mouth and leaned in to brush his lips over hers. "Where should I start?"

She swallowed. "Anywhere you want."

"Good answer." He began fondling her breasts as he kissed his way along her jawline.

Her earrings tinkled as he nuzzled behind her ear and ran his tongue over the tender lobe. When he caught it in his teeth, he pinched her nipples and a tremor rippled through her core. She drew in a quick breath, unable to believe that she was that close to a climax.

Then tension eased as he nipped and nibbled his way along her collarbone, but when he reached her breast and licked the pebbled surface of her nipple, another tremor shook her. Slowly, he drew in the tip. Opening his mouth wider, he took in more as he began rhythmically sucking.

"Grady…" She began to pant. She was close now, so close. Almost…

Sucking harder, he slipped his hand under the elastic of her panties. One thrust of his fingers and she arched off the counter with a sharp cry as her orgasm crashed through her. Struggling to breathe, she begged him to hold her before she fell.

Strong arms came around her and she rested her head against his broad shoulder. "That was some…kiss."

He chuckled. "Needed to give you something to remember me by while I took my shower."

"Please don't shower."

"No, really, I need to."

"You don't." Raising her head, she looked into his eyes. "On the way over, I got turned on just breathing in the raw masculinity of you. Don't shower, Grady. Just take me to bed."

6

GRADY WASN'T ABOUT to argue. After pulling off Sapphire's boots, jeans and panties, he carried her back to the bedroom, which was a trick because his cock felt stiff as a welding torch and he couldn't walk worth a damn. But having her naked in his arms was worth the pain in his crotch.

No woman had ever told him she loved the smell of his sweat. His job left him that way every day and he'd always assumed that he'd better clean up before he climbed into bed with a girlfriend. Apparently, Sapphire didn't care about that. In fact, she actually wanted him to take her without showering off the evidence of his labor. One more reason to assume they were right for each other.

He laid her on the bed and once again his thoughts went to the possibilities of a four-poster. Now that he knew Sapphire had sexual adventure in her soul, he had a feeling she'd like some of his ideas. But as he pulled off his boots and shucked his jeans and briefs, he only cared about the basics for now.

While he'd undressed, she'd tossed aside the lacy throw pillows and pushed the coverlet to the foot of the bed. Watching the process as her breasts moved seductively and her bottom occasionally swiveled in his direction had turned his cock into a heat-seeking missile. He approached the bed with a single goal.

She lay on her side, her head propped on her hand and her gaze focused on his package. She cleared her throat. "Very nice."

"I need to dress it up before it heads to the party."

She opened her other hand to reveal a foil packet resting on her palm. "Will this do?"

That was when he noticed a box on the lamp table that he'd sworn hadn't been there the first time he'd walked into this room. "Where'd the box come from?"

"I hid it under the bed in case Gandalf put up a fuss and we didn't get to do this."

He found that hilarious. He couldn't help grinning. "Are you saying that the unused box sitting there would have depressed you?"

"Wouldn't it have depressed *you*?"

"Come to think of it, yes. Thanks for hiding it. But Gandalf is obviously sound asleep, so I'll take that and make good use of it." As he started to pluck it from her hand, she pulled it away and sat up.

"I have a better idea. Come closer and I'll put it on." She moved to the edge of the bed.

He felt as if he could come just looking at her. "It'll be faster if I do it." And he needed fast.

"It'll be more fun if I do it. Come on over here." She tore the packet open and set it beside her.

He stepped within reach and she grasped his cock the way she might hold a hammer. Matter of fact, he probably could drive nails right now. His chest heaved. "Make it quick."

A slow smile greeted that remark. "What if I want to kiss you first?"

"Sapphire, no. I'm too close. I'll—" *Come.* She took away his power of speech the moment she licked away the drop of moisture trembling on the tip.

That was only her first move. Holding him firmly, she closed her lips over the sensitive head and began a slow slide. His cock touched the back of her throat and he clenched his hands, jaw, even his toes to keep from pouring everything he had into her mouth. By damn, he wasn't going to come until he was buried inside her sweet body.

She tested him. He called on restraint he didn't know he had as she licked and sucked. Oh, yeah, and massaged his tight balls. He regretted bragging about his stamina, although he couldn't imagine a man alive who could easily withstand this. But they'd probably love to try. He loved it, too, despite that the humiliation if he failed would be tough to endure.

About the time he was ready to surrender, she drew back. Cool air wafted over his wet cock and helped him maintain control while she rolled on the condom.

She lay back on the bed. "Now."

Her husky voice hummed in his ears as he climbed onto the mattress and leaned over her. "You're lucky I didn't come."

"You're lucky I didn't make you."

"Oh, so that's how it is?" Braced on his forearms, he settled himself between her thighs, poised at the entrance to paradise.

Her turquoise eyes gleamed with a combination of mischief and desire. "I decided to be nice. I knew how much you wanted this."

"And you don't?" He pushed in a short way and

paused while his heart threatened to beat itself right out of his chest. He was about to make love to a woman who fulfilled all his fantasies.

"I might be slightly interested."

"I think you are." He held himself right there, teasing her with the possibilities. Then he leaned down until his lips almost touched hers. "I think you are *very* interested." He gave her an openmouthed kiss with plenty of tongue until she moaned and clutched his hips in an attempt to bring him closer.

Somehow he managed to resist, although every instinct shouted at him to sink into her heat. She was a challenge and he loved a challenge. Taunting each other made sex fun and she was good at that. But so was he.

Slowly, he broke away from the seductive kiss. "What do you want, Sapphire?"

She let go of his hips so she could drag his head down. Then she murmured a very earthy two-word suggestion in his ear.

"I can do that." And he drove in deep. He hadn't expected her to come with one thrust, but she did. Arching her back, she shuddered in the grip of a climax that rolled over his cock. He gritted his teeth against the need to answer with a climax of his own. He wanted to give her one more.

He waited until she'd caught her breath. Then, as she lay soft and pliant beneath him, he began a relaxed, undemanding rhythm.

She looked up at him and smiled. "Now you're showing off."

"Uh-huh." He kept moving.

"I don't need another orgasm."

"But wouldn't it be nice?" He increased the pace.

Her eyes darkened and her body tensed. "I don't believe this."

"Believe it." He gulped for air as he struggled not to tumble over the edge. "You're going to come again."

Her thighs trembled. "You, too."

"Yeah, me, too." He finally slipped the leash on his control, and as he pumped rapidly, he knew his release was just around the corner. Damn, this was good. Her hips rose to meet each stroke. Any second now they'd—

The piercing meow from behind the bathroom door penetrated his passion-soaked brain. He paused midthrust.

"Gandalf." Sapphire's voice was strained.

"Yeah."

"We—" She gasped. "We should stop."

"Hell, no." And he pounded into her until they both came in a glorious rush. The cat's yowls intermingled with their cries, which guaranteed that he'd never forget the moment. But he wouldn't have anyway. A guy didn't forget his first time with his soul mate.

Gandalf continued his serenade as Grady's brain slowly stopped spinning and his breathing returned to normal. Propped on his forearms, he gazed into Sapphire's flushed face. He wanted to say something tender and significant, but he hesitated.

For one thing, it would lose something with the cat wailing in the background. For another, he'd started to mention his belief that they were meant for each other earlier, when they were in the kitchen. Her decision to invite him home with her had made him think it might be time.

But she'd interrupted him. She'd also looked scared, like she didn't want to hear that sort of thing. He had to admit it was a little soon to get mushy, even if she was the woman he'd dreamed of during the long winter nights in Alaska.

He might be better off not telling her that yet. She probably needed time to catch up before he came out with such dramatic statements. She clearly liked having sex with him, so he'd concentrate on that aspect for the time being.

Smiling, he looked into her eyes. "That was memorable."

"No kidding." She smiled back. "Still breaking new ground."

She had no idea how true that was. Taking a firm grip on the condom, he eased away from her. "I'll go in there and see if I can settle him down."

"He seems to have forgotten your agreement."

"I intend to remind him." He glanced at her. "And I'll also take a quick shower."

She laughed softly. "If you must."

She looked incredible lying there, all rosy and mussed. "Wish you could join me."

"I have a feeling that wouldn't turn out the way you hope. I'll take one upstairs. And order our pizza."

"Oh, yeah. Pizza." He suddenly realized he was ravenous. "Get an extra large, okay?" He started toward the bathroom.

"I will. Be careful he doesn't sneak out."

"No worries." Getting through the bathroom door without letting Gandalf out or losing his hold on the condom took coordination, but luckily, he'd been blessed with a fair amount of it. He blocked the cat with his foot and kept him back while he slipped inside the bathroom and closed the door.

Gandalf rubbed against his leg and purred.

"Yeah, you and I need to have a little talk." Grady

disposed of the condom and turned on the shower. "Right after I clean up a bit." He grabbed a washcloth off the towel rack, pulled back the cat-themed curtain of the tub shower and stepped under the spray. It was a little weak but he figured that was because Sapphire was using the one upstairs.

That brought up images of her naked in the shower, which made him think of all the fun things they could do together if they were sharing that experience. He had to stop thinking about that or he'd be hard again, and he had to deal with this cat. That was okay, because Gandalf needed him right now and befriending the cat might have tipped the scales in his favor with Sapphire.

He stuck his head under the water and took a little of her shampoo to lather his hair. She might love his manly scent but he was so over it. As he ducked under the spray again to rinse away the suds, Gandalf meowed.

"Taking a shower here, cat. Can't pet you."

The rustle of the curtain was followed by a thump. When Grady turned around and wiped his eyes, there was Gandalf sitting in the tub staring at him with his blue eyes. The cat seemed oblivious to the water pelting down on him.

"What the hell? Aren't you supposed to hate water?"

Gandalf padded over and began licking Grady's leg. His tongue felt like sandpaper but it tickled, too.

"You are one weird feline, Gandalf. I suppose if I lifted you out, you'd hop right back in. Besides, you're wet now, so you'd make a mess. Can't have that." He quickly used the washcloth while Gandalf continued to lick his leg. By the time Grady turned off the shower, the cat was pretty wet.

Maybe this wasn't all bad. Leaning down, he stroked the washcloth over the cat's long hair, which had dark-

ened to charcoal under the spray. He'd picked out the
burrs earlier while Gandalf was eating tuna and now he
was able to make some progress on the matted places.

Gandalf stood tolerantly while he was being tended
to. He didn't protest when Grady grabbed a towel and
bundled him into it. Instead he started to purr.

Grady stepped out of the tub, then sat on the bath mat
and gently massaged the cat with the towel. "I can't decide if you're the most maddening animal in the world
or the most fascinating." After rubbing the cat until he
was damp-dry, he turned him loose. "You finish the
job, okay?"

Sure enough, Gandalf began grooming himself.

The towel Grady had used for the cat was covered
with hair, so he folded it up and took a different one
for himself. As he dried off, he talked to Gandalf. "I
thought we had an understanding, buddy. I have something special going with Sapphire and I don't appreciate
it when you make noise in the middle of a most excellent roll in the hay."

The cat ignored him.

"You may not be able to relate now that you've lost
your family jewels, but for those of us who still have
ours, using them is important." He watched Gandalf
lick his paw and swipe it over his whiskers. Cute move.
"So even if you don't get why I like that activity, I'm
asking you to respect my need for it. If you promise
not to meow to get my attention, I promise to check on
you whenever I'm not having sex with the lady. Okay?"

Gandalf looked up and blinked.

"I'll take that as your word of honor." He wrapped
the towel around his hips. "I'm going back out there,
and depending on when the pizza's being delivered, I

could become intimately involved again, if you take my meaning."

The cat made that funny little noise that was somewhere between a meow and a purr.

"I think you do. Be a good boy." He slipped out the door and closed it securely. When he turned, Sapphire stood there wearing a silky green robe and a smile. "Well, hello there." He took note of the way the material draped and decided she wasn't wearing a bra, which might also mean she wasn't wearing panties, either.

"Hello, yourself." She glanced at the towel around his hips. "Apparently, you took that shower you were so dead set on."

"I did. So when's the pizza supposed to arrive?"

Her smiled widened. "They're swamped. It'll be at least an hour."

"You don't seem very upset by the delay."

"I'm not."

"Were you by chance eavesdropping on my conversation with Gandalf?"

"Oh, I might have heard a reference to timing of the pizza regarding certain other activities."

His cock rose to attention, which couldn't be disguised by a towel. "And how do you feel about that?"

She laughed. "Regardless, I already know how you feel about it."

"That's the thing about guys. We put it all out there." He stepped closer and loosened the tie on her robe. "Girls, not so much. So guys have to learn to read the subtle signs."

"Like what?"

He ran a finger over her cheekbone. "A slight flush on your skin, a widening of your pupils, a catch in your breath."

She shivered. "What else?"

"Puckered nipples, unless it's cold." He brushed his knuckles over the hunter green silk covering her breasts. "Are you cold?"

"No."

"Then judging from what I feel through this material, you're quite possibly aroused. But there's only one way to be sure."

"What's that?"

Parting her robe, he reached between her thighs. His fingers came away wet. He stroked her bottom lip, moistening it with her juices. "Dead giveaway."

She looked up at him with passion-glazed eyes. "And what are you going to do about it?" Her breathy question was barely audible.

"I have a few ideas." As he backed her toward the bed, his towel fell away.

"So I see."

"I'm saving that for later." He cupped her face in both hands and nibbled on her mouth. "I really am hungry and since the pizza won't be here for a while, I'll have to make do with you."

"How you talk." Her voice quavered.

"That's not all I can do with my mouth."

She moaned. "I know."

"Not really." He pushed gently on her shoulders. "But if you'll sit back and relax, I'll be happy to show you."

She sank down to the edge of the mattress and he dropped to his knees on the plush carpet beside the bed. "I don't think you need this anymore." He slipped her robe over her arms and it drifted to the bed to fan around her, making her the focal point of delicious pleasure.

"I love your breasts." Cupping them, he tasted each nipple and rolled it over the flat of his tongue.

She shuddered. "That feels good."

"And this?" He trailed kisses down to her navel and circled it with the tip of his tongue.

She drew in a sharp breath. "That, too."

Coaxing her thighs apart, he blew on her damp curls. "Like that?"

"Mmm."

He scooted lower and flicked his tongue over the sweet spot nesting among those curls. "That?"

She moaned.

"I'll take that as a yes." Slowly, he began his exploration, beginning with her clit. He made love to it with his tongue. He loved the taste of her, loved the way he made her whimper. Then he grazed that pulsing trigger point with his teeth and finally drew it into his mouth.

Her breathing grew faster with every stage. Sliding his hands under her bottom, he tilted her hips because he needed… Yes, there. She was like velvet and so hot, so drenched with desire. He explored and probed as she clutched his head and made soft mewling sounds.

He knew the exact moment when she surrendered completely. Her knees fell apart and she gave up all pretense of modesty. Throwing open the gates, she invited him to plunder at will. He didn't hesitate.

He took all she had to give—licking and sucking until the flow of her nectar flooded his tongue and her cries filled the room. He pressed on until she came again, her hips bucking and her fingertips digging into his scalp. She called his name. Ah, how he loved that she'd called his name.

"Enough." Panting, she leaned down and kissed the top of his head. "Please stop before I die of pleasure."

He placed kisses along her damp thighs before he

rose up and kissed her fully on the mouth. Their lips met in a sensuous dance flavored by her orgasms.

The taste of sex seemed to inspire her, because she closed her hand around his still-rigid cock. She broke away from the erotic kiss. "I can't leave you like this."

"Sure you can."

"I can't. But I don't think I can…reciprocate."

"That's okay. I'll be fine."

"No, it's not fair." Releasing him, she wiggled back up on the bed. "Do me, Grady. I may not have the strength to participate a whole lot, but at least I'll know that I didn't leave you hanging."

He smiled. "Honestly, we don't have to—"

"Yes, we do! I'll feel so guilty if you don't grab a condom and climb aboard." She held out her hand. "Come on, cowboy. You know you want to."

"Nope. I can wait."

"But I'm all warmed up." She put her other hand between her thighs and began to touch herself. "You'll have a good time."

He had only so much willpower. "Yeah, I sure will." He had a condom on in no time and his body hummed with anticipation. "I'll make it quick."

"Take as long as you like." She bent her knees to give him a perfect view of heaven. "Now, come on and make yourself feel good."

He'd defy any man to resist such an offer. Moving over her, he thrust into her orgasm-slicked channel with a groan of pure happiness.

"I told you you'd like it."

"That was never in doubt." He put his weight on his outstretched hands this time so he could watch her breasts quiver each time he shoved home. "I want you to come, too."

"Don't think about that. This is for you. Do whatever makes you feel good."

"I broke that habit a long time ago."

"Then fall back into it." She clutched his butt cheeks. "Show me what you were like at seventeen. Go for the gusto. I want to see you lose it."

Temptation shot arrows of fire through his blood. "Oh, Sapphire."

"I dare you."

No one had dared him in a very long time, especially not a naked woman who was massaging his butt and taunting him to unleash the hedonist he knew he could be. Heart thundering, he withdrew. "Okay. Turn over."

She looked surprised, but she did it.

"Get on your hands and knees."

She did that, too.

He watched her through a red haze of lust. "Lean on your forearms and lift your hips."

"How's that?"

"Good. Move your knees apart. There." Positioning himself behind her, he dipped his fingers into her entrance. She was drenched.

"Hurry," she murmured. "I think I might come."

That was all he needed to know. One thrust and he was buried to the hilt, his thighs touching hers.

"Go for it." She sounded slightly desperate.

He turned himself loose, driving into her again and again. The slap of his thighs against hers blended with the liquid rhythm of each stroke. Their ragged breathing became moans that turned into urgent cries.

This wasn't about making love. It was about raw, unfettered sex and he reveled in it. She'd given him permission to submerge himself in carnality and he welcomed it with each frenzied thrust of his cock.

He didn't wait for her, because she'd said not to. He came with a roar of triumph as he slammed into her one last time and held himself there as he pulsed within her. Vaguely, he realized she'd come, too, and her spasms milked him until he sank against her, spent and panting.

She dragged in a breath. "Good."

"So…good." He steadied her as he eased them down to the mattress so they could lie spooned together. Eventually, he'd have to move and deal with the condom. Sooner or later the pizza would arrive. But for now he just wanted to hold her. He felt as if he could do that forever.

7

BY SOME MIRACLE, they managed to get out of bed before the pizza arrived, but Sapphire had wondered if they'd make it. Originally, she'd thought that an hour for fun and games was more than enough time, but she hadn't counted on the level of erotic energy she and Grady generated. Their last episode had developed an orgy-like quality that could have gone on for hours.

She'd fully expected Gandalf to interrupt them but he hadn't. Maybe his exhaustion had finally caught up with him and he'd zonked out. That would be great, because in spite of their last sexual episode, she and Grady weren't finished with each other. The air still crackled whenever they exchanged a glance.

But as if by mutual agreement, they'd taken chairs on opposite sides of the kitchen table while they ate pizza and sipped cans of beer she happened to have in the fridge. They'd have to stretch to make contact. Grady's legs were long enough to play footsie under the table but he didn't do that, either.

She hoped the extra-large pizza with everything on it would be enough food. He was a big guy and he'd had an active day plus an even more active night.

"I have ice cream," she said when the pizza was gone.

"Great. I'd love some." He tipped back his head to get the last swallow of his beer.

She longed to go over and kiss the tanned column of his throat. Then she'd move on to his chest, where the little red dots were fading. He must be a fast healer, after all. She wouldn't doubt it. He was a healthy, vital male with a lusty outlook on life. No wonder she craved him.

He set down the empty can and met her gaze. "Or maybe you'd rather have a different kind of dessert." His eyebrows lifted and the corner of his mouth curved just enough to make him look like a rogue, especially when she caught the glitter of desire in his eyes.

Her body tightened in response. Oh, yes, she wanted what he promised with that subtle smile even though it hadn't been that long since the last time. She couldn't remember being this obsessed with a guy. Some restraint might be in order so she wouldn't get carried away. "Let's slow it down a little."

"You sure? Just now you looked quite interested in another round."

"I am."

He scraped back his chair. "Then come with me." He laughed. "Or come first and then come with me. It's all good."

"Yes, it is, but there's something to be said for delayed gratification."

He stood and walked behind her chair. "I'm not a big fan of delayed gratification." Drawing her hair aside, he leaned down and nibbled behind her ear. "I love that you've left these sexy earrings in the whole time. They turn me on."

Closing her eyes, she tilted her head to give him greater access to her sensitized skin. With a murmur of approval, he slid his hand under the collar of her robe to fondle her breast. "Come back to bed," he crooned as he brushed his thumb over her nipple. "Unless you want to do it right here on the table. I tucked a condom in my pocket."

She smiled. "You did not."

"I did." He nuzzled her throat. "I wanted to be ready when you were ready, whenever and wherever that turned out to be."

"Grady…this is insane." But she no longer cared about restraint. He'd thought to tuck a condom in his pocket in case they decided to do it on the kitchen table. And why not, when they both wanted to? Then her phone rang.

Grady's caress moved lower and his voice rumbled in her ear. "Let it go to voice mail."

"It's my mother."

"All the more reason." He reached between her thighs, touching her with knowing fingers. "You're in no position to talk to your mother."

She groaned. "I have to. We scheduled this call. If I don't answer, she'll worry."

"In that case…" He slowly withdrew his hand and kissed her cheek. "I'll check on Gandalf."

"Sorry." Pulling her robe back together, she glanced at him as she rose on wobbly legs.

His fly strained against the pressure of his erect cock, but he smiled as if that was of no consequence. "Unless you plan to kick me out within the next hour, we'll have another shot at it."

"I'm not kicking you out." She wanted him to stay here for the entire week, but she hadn't thought it through very well. Besides her pledge to Amethyst, she'd also promised her mother that she wouldn't date any more artists. Her mom and her sister had taken the brunt of her angst after all four breakups.

"Then I'll catch you later." He left the kitchen.

Her phone had stopped ringing long before she made it to the counter. She took several deep breaths before calling her mother back.

Her mom answered immediately. "Hi, sweetie! I just left you a message."

"I didn't listen to it. Just called you instead." She tucked the phone against her ear while she cinched the belt on her robe. Silly, but she felt the need to do it. "So what have you decided? The weaving or the sculpture?" A few local artists including her mom were donating finished works for the silent auction.

"The weaving. I've been thinking about Grady Magee."

Sapphire choked and began to cough as she struggled to breathe.

"Honey, are you okay?"

"Fine," she managed to say in a strangled voice. "Swallowed wrong."

"You got that from your father. Scares me to death when he does it. Anyway, Grady's the only other sculptor in the show, and while my work is totally different, I'd like him to have the honor of being the only one."

"I'm sure he'd share the spotlight."

"Probably. He was a nice boy in school, so I'm sure he's become a very nice man."

Oh, yeah. Sapphire swallowed carefully so she wouldn't give a repeat performance.

"To think that kid became a successful artist. I never would have predicted it, but he's a great role model for my students, especially the boys. He came in yesterday, right?"

"He did, and I—"

"I assume you've spent some time with him, then."

"I have, Mom, and that's something I need to talk to you about."

"Please don't tell me he's arrogant. You were sort of quiet when I said he'd probably become a nice man, so maybe he's turned into a jerk and you didn't want to say so. Quick success can do that to a person. If he's arrogant, then I won't ask him to come back and speak to my students in the fall."

Oh, boy. All hope of keeping the situation under control vanished. She'd never dreamed that her mom would see the potential in having a Sheridan High alum who'd made a name for himself speak to her art classes. "He's not a jerk," she said. "He's great and you should definitely ask him."

"Fabulous! I know he visits his foster parents every now and then, so I could coordinate with his plans. I was surprised when Molly Radcliffe told me he was staying with her and Ben this time. I thought for sure he'd be out at Thunder Mountain."

"When the academy's going, it's crazy busy out there. He didn't want to get in the way."

"Then he could certainly stay here in the fall if he needed a place to crash. I'd love a chance to talk with him. If he's willing, we could set up a visit each semester."

"That would be terrific." Now Sapphire felt greedy for keeping this paragon to herself. Had she really thought they could hide away and have sex all week without the entire town knowing about it? In the privacy of her bedroom, locked in his arms, she'd thought exactly that.

"I've heard via the art grapevine that he's working on some top secret project and shouldn't be disturbed, so I'll wait until the welcome reception to talk with him about it. Of course, I could ask Ben and Molly if I could drop by some evening. I mean, the guy can't be working all day and all night, can he?"

"Mom, he's not at Ben and Molly's." She wondered if Grady had thought of calling them to explain the change of plans. Probably not, since he'd been as preoccupied with Gandalf—and sex—as she had.

"Then where is he?"

"Here."

"You mean *here* as in your house?"

"Yes. A new cat arrived at feeding time tonight and he's not feral. He took to Grady right away and Grady didn't want to leave him at the shelter, so we brought him over here."

"But your sister's allergic!"

"I know, so he's closed up in my bathroom." She found herself talking very fast. "It should be okay if I keep him confined there. I checked him for fleas and mites and tomorrow I'll take him to the shelter vet to make sure there are no issues. After that I may—"

"So the cat's in the bathroom safe and sound."

"Yes, and Grady wants to stay with him until we find out whether he has a home or not."

"So Grady's in your bathroom with the cat?"

"Um, sometimes. Right now he is."

"He'll come out with cat hair on him. You can't let him roam around and sit on the furniture after he's spent time with the cat. Or if you do, you'll have to vacuum that house within an inch of its life."

"Good point. I'll make sure he doesn't spread cat hair around." Maybe she needed to keep him confined to her bedroom, after all.

Her mother was silent for a beat. "Sapphire Jane, what's going on?"

"Grady and I are...involved."

Her mom was silent for a moment. "But he's an artist."

"I know."

"I can't say I'm surprised that you're attracted to him. I've seen him on TV and he's a good-looking guy, exactly your type, or what used to be your type before you swore off artists."

"I said I wouldn't date them anymore. But we're not exactly dating."

Her mother laughed. "Guess not. You skipped right over that part."

"I don't know if I can explain it." Or, more accurately, *how* to explain it. She could tell her mom that she was sleeping with Grady but she didn't want to admit it was only about sex. Saying that to her mom felt weird.

"Honey, you don't have to explain. You're a grown woman free to do what you want in that department. I won't hold you to that statement you made before he showed up and changed your mind."

"He hasn't changed my mind."

"Not yet."

"He won't."

"Whatever you say, sweetie. Anyway, I'd love for you to bring him to dinner tomorrow night."

"I'll ask him and let you know."

"Good."

"Oh, and if we come to dinner, could you please not tell Dad that Grady's staying with me?"

"I won't, but your father's not an idiot. He'll figure it out."

"Yeah, well, I still don't want you to tell him."

"I won't. Good night, honey."

"Night, Mom." She disconnected and stared at the phone. So her mother thought Grady would change her mind about getting involved with an artist. She couldn't allow that to happen. This thing between them was spontaneous and fun. Avoiding any talk of future plans was the only way to keep it that way.

Her mother's brainstorm of inviting Grady to speak at the high school could complicate matters. Oh, well, they could burn that bridge when they got to it. In the meantime, she had some things to discuss with the man of the hour.

She walked into the bedroom and over to the bathroom door, where light shone underneath. Once again cat and man were having a conversation. This close to the door, she could catch most of what Grady was saying. What Gandalf was saying was anybody's guess.

"So good job on staying cool while you're temporarily in lockup, buddy. I'll be back to check on you next time there's a break in the action, okay?"

She had a fair idea what action he was talking about. She knocked lightly on the door. "I hate to interrupt, but can I see you for a minute?"

His light chuckle tickled her nerve endings. "We covered this. A minute is no longer sufficient."

"I'm not talking about having sex."

"Thank God, because doing it is a whole lot better than talking about it. Unless you're referring to phone sex, where you talk and do at the same time. I suppose that could be interesting for a change of pace, but it's not my first choice."

"Then since what I have to say has nothing to do with sex, we could just talk through the bathroom door."

"Nah." Rustling sounds were followed by a plaintive

meow. "Sorry, Gandalf, lap time is over. She may think we aren't talking about sex, but when you consider the past twenty-four hours, it's clear that sex underlies everything. Go have a little snooze and I'll be back later." The light went out and Grady slipped through the door. This time he was wearing his hat. "You rang?"

"Take off your clothes."

He grinned. "I like where this is going."

"It's not what you think. My mother pointed out that you'll come out of the bathroom covered in cat hair and I shouldn't let you walk around the house in those clothes."

He unzipped his jeans. "So walking around naked is a better option? I've always liked your mom but now she's a real favorite of mine."

"That's good, because she's invited us both to dinner tomorrow night."

"Oh, yeah? That's great. I'm in." He started pulling off his jeans.

"You wouldn't mind?"

"No, it'll be great to see her again. I only met your dad a couple of times but any guy who can make money with a saxophone has my admiration."

"She already knows we're having sex."

"Oh?" He paused with one leg still stuck in his pants. "Does she have your bedroom bugged?"

"No, I told her."

"Interesting. Is your dad gonna threaten me with a shotgun?"

"Not unless you say something insulting about his jazz trio."

"Wouldn't dream of it." He took off his hat and laid it brim-up on the dresser. "I didn't want to take a chance

Gandalf would chew on this. It's old but we've been through a lot together."

She found that endearing, but then, many things about Grady were endearing. Her previous lovers had been charming, too, until one day they weren't.

He stripped off his briefs. "Are we supposed to burn these or what?"

"Would you let me?" Seeing him standing there in all his glory, she was tempted.

"If it's that or give up sex with you, sure. Light 'em up. Just not my hat. I'm very attached to it. But take these." He held them out. "They're dead to me."

"I think tossing them in the washing machine is good enough. Then you'll have something clean to wear in the morning." She tucked his clothes under her arm.

"And not a single thing to wear for the rest of the night. Oh, darn."

She thought about letting him stay that way because he was so pretty to look at. Greek statues had nothing on him. But having no clothes meant he'd be naked in an emergency or when he went in to check on Gandalf. "I have another bathrobe."

"Yeah, no. Not wearing a lady's robe. Thanks, but no thanks."

"It's black and kind of big on me."

"Does it have a sash like yours?"

"Yep. Very simple design. Velour. Not the least bit girlie."

"Pockets?"

"I think so."

"Then I'll take it. I've been thinking we should sit out on your front porch while we have ice cream."

"Really?" She thought he'd forgotten about the dessert she'd offered.

"Really. I live in a barn, literally, and we have no front porch, so naturally, I wish I had one. I'd have fun sitting on yours and watching the world go by, but I'd better not do it wearing just my hat."

She laughed. "We don't have a lot of traffic on this road and the neighbors are usually inside watching TV by now, but yes, sitting naked on the porch might be pushing it."

"And there's a chill in the air."

"That, too." She headed over to her closet, grabbed the robe off its hanger and tossed it to him. "One other thing. What about Ben and Molly?"

He blew out a breath. "Right. I need to call but what should I say?"

"Not what I told my mother, although they may draw the same conclusion no matter what you say."

He shoved his arms into the sleeves of the robe. "I thought about it while I was in there with Gandalf. What if I said that a stray cat brought us together and then we discovered all the things we have in common and want to take the week to explore them?"

"They'll still know it's about sex."

"Absolutely they will." Although the robe didn't begin to cover his chest, the bottom came together just enough to keep him from getting arrested. "But if I don't come right out and announce we're swinging from the chandeliers, we can all save face when I pick up my stuff tomorrow." He hesitated. "I made a leap there. I never asked if you wanted me here for the duration."

"I do." The hint of vulnerability in his brown eyes touched her more deeply than she wanted it to. She brushed a quick kiss over his mouth. "Call them and then go pick your ice-cream flavors while I start a load of laundry."

"There are choices?" He sounded like a kid in a candy store.

"Of course there are," she called over her shoulder as she headed for the laundry room. "I take my ice cream seriously."

"Me, too! See, I'm not lying to Ben and Molly. We do need to explore these things."

Technically, they didn't, she thought as she measured soap and set the dial on the washer. Two people with chemistry, which they had in spades, could have very satisfying sex without ever exploring their ice-cream preferences, or their love of porch sitting or their similar tastes in pizza. Sharing this info might make the connection a little more interesting but it wasn't essential.

At least, that was what she told herself until she walked back into the kitchen and found him with all four ice-cream cartons lined up on the counter. He was studying them with great intensity, which she found adorable. "Did you talk to Ben and Molly?"

He turned with a grin. "I got Ben. He sounded like he wanted to bust out laughing while I stumbled through my explanation. He said to tell you hi."

"He's a good guy." She gestured toward the four cartons. "Find anything you like?"

"I love them all. What are the chances?"

She shrugged. "They're popular flavors."

"Come on. Blueberry cheesecake? I've never known anybody else who loved it enough to buy a whole carton. Or did your sister get that one?"

She wished she could blame that choice on Amethyst, but her sister could take it or leave it. She wasn't even a big fan of ice cream in general. Sapphire was, and blueberry cheesecake had been her favorite for years. "No, I did."

He popped off the lid. "That's my pick, then. There's plenty for both of us, if it's your favorite, too."

She decided there was no harm in admitting they loved the same ice cream. "It is. I'll get us a couple of bowls."

"Why bother? Grab two spoons and we're good."

"You're okay sharing the carton?" She wasn't convinced she was. The symbolism, sort of like a soda with two straws, worried her.

He smiled. "We've already shared something way more intimate than ice cream."

"True." The reminder flooded her with a warm, achy feeling. It didn't make her desperate to have him right now, though. She could wait. She could also sit with him on the porch and share a carton of ice cream without imagining it as a prelude to a complication. "I'll get the spoons."

8

"I DON'T SPEND enough time outdoors." Grady listened to the crickets chirping in the bushes next to the front porch as he rocked lazily back and forth. "As a kid I was always outside. Porch sitting at Thunder Mountain is an evening tradition, at least when the weather's nice."

"The porch is one of the main reasons Amethyst and I decided to rent this house. We bought the rockers the same day we moved in." She passed him the container of ice cream. "Your turn."

"Thanks. This is delicious. I've been so busy lately that I've scrounged whatever food I could find in the kitchen. I ran out of ice cream weeks ago."

"That can happen when you're involved in your work."

"Yep, and I get to the point where I don't care what I eat. Liam used to stock food and sometimes cook, but summer's his busy rafting schedule, plus now there's Hope."

"Hope for what?"

He laughed. "Sorry. Hope's the woman Liam fell for this summer. I keep forgetting everybody around here doesn't know her." He took another spoonful of ice cream and sent the carton back to her. "She lives in Cody but she came up to Sheridan for Damon and Philomena's wedding in July."

"You mean the wedding where you gave them a ginormous sculpture that has folks driving by their house just to see it?"

"They do?"

"I'm surprised Damon hasn't told you. It's become a tourist attraction for anyone who loves art. It's not like there's a steady stream of cars, although if you get any more famous, that could happen."

Grady winced. "I hadn't thought of that angle. I hope they're not upset."

"More likely they're proud of being your friend."

"Damon's way more than a friend. He— Well, let's just say I wouldn't be where I am today if we hadn't been at Thunder Mountain together. He's the one who encouraged me to pursue a career in welding."

"He is? I didn't know that."

"Yeah." He leaned back in his chair. "I idolized the guy. Still do."

"Then he has even more reason to be proud. You're a big deal."

"I guess so. For the time being anyway." He'd never taken his success for granted and never would.

"I predict you'll have a long career. Your work has a timeless quality."

"Thanks for saying so, but people can lose interest. I've seen it happen to others—artists with a truckload of talent. That's why I'm glad Liam's been investing the money for me. I don't have much ability when it comes to that but he does. He says if I don't buy any mansions or yachts, I should be fine for quite a while."

She laughed. "Do you want a mansion or a yacht?"

"Not much reason to have a yacht in Wyoming."

"A mansion, then?"

"Can't think what I'd do with one. The barn is perfect—living space upstairs and working space downstairs. I just want to keep doing what I love."

"Me, too." She handed him the carton. "I'm done. You can have the rest."

They'd turned the porch light off, so he couldn't see how much was left, but a quick jab with his spoon told him there was quite a bit. "You haven't eaten your share."

"I had enough. You're the ice-cream-deprived person, not me. Enjoy yourself."

"Thank you. Very generous." He tucked into it. Their quiet conversation had been great, but sex had never been far from his mind. Savoring the creamy texture of blueberry cheesecake on his tongue reminded him of other sensuous treats, ones within arm's reach. "I'm enjoying myself quite a bit tonight thanks to you."

"Right back atcha."

"Glad to hear it. That's the really great thing about sex." He paused. "Can I discuss this on your porch or will your neighbors hear me and be shocked?"

"They won't hear you over the sound of their TVs."

"Good to know." He didn't really want to discuss sex. He felt like doing it. Right after he finished this most excellent ice cream.

Sapphire rocked slowly back and forth. "The folks on both sides are avid fans of several shows. They've tried talking to me about them but I've only caught a glimpse of an episode or two."

"Too busy working, right?"

"Exactly. Some nights I stay at the barn and others I'm here sketching and planning out what I'll do the next day. Or reading up on new glazes or a tool that creates unusual effects."

"So you work at the barn at night?"

"Once in a while. Would you like to while you're here?"

"If I need extra time for Rosie's sculpture, you bet. I didn't know how you'd feel about me staying after hours."

"Fine with me. I might keep you company."

"I'd like that. Having you working next to me today was stimulating. And surprisingly, not in a sexual way."

"I know."

He glanced over at her. Soft light came through the curtains over the living room windows, but she had her back to the windows, so her face was in the shadow. "How do you know?"

"Because I watched you submerge yourself in your work today. Your entire attitude changed. I doubt you would have noticed if I'd stripped down and performed the Dance of the Seven Veils."

He nearly spewed ice cream. Instead he managed to swallow it. "I wouldn't go that far."

"I would. I admire that quality and that's another reason you'll make it in this business. You're focused."

"Thank you." He did get into the zone when he worked. If anyone had asked him whether he could stay in that zone while a sexy woman sat at a potter's wheel a few feet away, he would have said no. But he'd proved today that he could. Knowing that she was also absorbed in her project might have had something to do with it.

But they weren't working now and their dessert was nearly gone. He hadn't forgotten that she wore nothing but a silk robe. He wore nothing but the robe she'd loaned him and he'd shoved a condom in the pocket. Having sex out here carried the risk of discovery, and yet she'd said the neighbors were all inside and glued to their TVs.

She continued to rock gently. "So I think we could work together in the barn some night while you're here without worrying that we'd be distracted by sex. Instead we'd inspire each other."

He agreed, but at the moment he was inspired to lift her onto the porch railing and slide his aching cock into her welcoming body. The railing looked sturdy enough. He also had some softened ice cream left in the bottom of the container and he had a great idea for how to use it.

"You're awfully quiet over there, Grady. You okay?"

"I'm super." He licked the spoon and stuck it in his other pocket. Then he grasped the carton, left his rocker and crouched in front of hers. "But I have a huge favor to ask." He caressed the silk covering her knee.

She laughed. "Why do I get the feeling this has something to do with sex?"

"Because it does." He liked the way silk slid easily away from bare skin. He cupped her bare knee and massaged gently. "I have some ice cream left but it's almost melted. That's an anticlimactic way to finish it off. Licking it from your warm breasts would be a much better ending for this carton of blueberry cheesecake."

"Sounds messy." But her voice trembled.

"Is that a yes or a no?"

"It's a maybe." Her breathing had changed, too.

"You'll be amazed at how neat I can be. I don't want to waste a single drop of my favorite ice cream."

"Was this your plan when you suggested eating our dessert on the porch?"

"Not exactly, but hosing down a porch is an easier cleanup than any place inside the house."

"So some of the ice cream was ultimately going to end up on me?"

"Only if you said yes."

She swallowed. "Okay. Yes."

"Hot damn."

"But we can't get ice cream on these chair cushions. They're half Amethyst's."

"I had a different plan anyway. I thought you could sit on the porch railing."

Her breath caught. "Facing the light from the living room."

"I need to see." He stroked her thigh.

"But a neighbor could come out and…"

"Probably won't happen."

"Probably not." She shivered.

"Are you afraid?"

She shook her head.

"Turned on?"

Her voice was low and sultry. "Yes."

Pulse hammering, he stood and offered his hand. Once he helped her out of the chair, it was a simple matter to boost her up on the railing at a spot where she could reach one of the spindled posts to steady herself.

Then he set the carton on the railing and cupped her cheek. As he leaned in for a kiss, he reached for her sash. He'd been tempted to untie it ever since she'd first appeared in the robe, and he'd fantasized about doing it all during their dinner of pizza and beer. But his plan to get that robe open had gone up in flames with her mother's phone call.

At last he could have the view he'd longed for. One quick tug and the robe hung loosely from her shoulders.

Breaking away from the kiss, he stepped back to view his handiwork. Her breasts peeked from the lapels, and with each ragged breath she took, the lapels edged farther apart. He decided to help that process along and swept them aside.

That left her completely covered on the street side but gloriously naked on his side. Her bare feet dangled and her thighs were slightly parted to give him a tantalizing glimpse of his ultimate goal.

If he moved an inch or so, the ambient light from the living room illuminated her smooth skin and luscious curves even more. The mellow glow highlighted the classic beauty of her body and he regretted never taking an art course of any kind. If he had, he'd have her pose so he could sketch her.

As it was, he didn't have a lot of confidence in his drawing ability. He used it to map out plans for sculptures but he had no illusions about the quality of those sketches. Galleries had requested them, even offered him crazy amounts of money, but he'd refused. He was self-taught and he knew his efforts were crude. He didn't want some half-baked representation of his work to circulate.

But just this once he wished that he had the training to re-create what he was seeing in some form, whether it was in charcoal, paint or clay. She might not agree to that. Or maybe she'd already allowed another artist the privilege. In some ways he knew her so well and in others he knew almost nothing.

Given time, he could fix that. He'd thought about the geographical barrier between them and he wouldn't let it be a problem. But first he had to be convinced that she wanted him as much as he wanted her.

Sexually, he knew she did. The evidence was right

in front of him. Her chest heaved with each shallow breath and even in this light he could tell the curls between her thighs were damp. She had the same thirst for sexual adventure that he did.

Emotionally, though, he wasn't so sure of her. Something was preventing her from opening up and he couldn't get a handle on it. It was still too soon to talk about deeper feelings, so he'd continue to capitalize on the one emotion that had worked from the beginning—lust.

He dipped his fingers in the carton to coat them with melted ice cream. Although the creamy substance wasn't frigid anymore, she might feel the chill. "Tell me if this is too cold."

She gasped as he began finger painting her breasts. "Too cold?"

"No. Startling. I've never been painted with ice cream before." She traced the path he'd taken and then sucked on her finger. "But I like it."

Heat surged through him and he considered abandoning the ice cream in favor of snapping on the condom and sliding into her. She was ready. He knew that from the way her body trembled whenever he touched her.

But if he gave up on the ice cream, he'd lose an element that had bonded them together. She might think loving the same flavor wasn't important, but he wasn't so sure. Sometimes a simple thing could be the sentimental link that made all the difference.

So he coated his fingers again and this time he did a more thorough job of covering her breasts. Licking her clean would take a while but he'd give it his best effort. Her nipples required extra attention because they seemed to collect more stickiness.

Finally, he resorted to sucking on each one for several seconds to make sure he'd removed every last bit of blueberry-cheesecake ice cream. By the time he finished, she was clutching the post with one hand and the railing with the other while she whimpered and moaned.

She was excited, no question. But fooling around with ice cream was different from full-out sex and he didn't know if she'd let him go that far. So he worked his way back to her mouth and kissed her thoroughly with plenty of tongue to gauge her level of arousal. She responded to the kiss with such enthusiasm that he was encouraged.

At last he gave up the pleasure of kissing her so he could broach the possibility of having sex in the great outdoors. He'd meant to be subtle about it.

Instead he blurted out his request in a gravelly voice worthy of a gangster movie. "I want you." He sucked in air. "Right here on the porch, sitting on the railing. Is that okay with you?"

"What if I fall in the bushes?"

"You won't. You'll be anchored to my cock at all times."

"Mmm." Keeping her hold on the post, she ran her free hand down his chest. She paused at the tie holding his robe closed, then yanked it free to reveal his extremely erect penis. Smiling, she lifted her gaze to his. "Got a raincoat in your pocket?"

He pulled out the condom.

Her eyes darkened and she took a firmer grip on the post. Shifting her position slightly, she opened her thighs. "Then you'd better dock that bad boy before you get arrested for flashing the neighbors."

After putting the condom on in record time, he reached inside her robe and grasped her hips. Once he had his bearings, he could have managed the next step blindfolded, but he gave in to temptation. He'd never watched his cock make that journey and tonight he wanted to see his first deep thrust. The sight was way more erotic than he'd imagined. He damn near came.

"Like the view, cowboy?" Her voice had become a husky drawl.

"Love it." He raised his head and registered the flush on her cheeks and the glitter in her eyes. "Best view in the world."

"Hold still and keep watching." Her breasts quivered as her breathing picked up speed. "Allow me to add to your viewing pleasure. Let's start here." She slowly sucked on her finger.

His cock twitched. Guaranteed that whatever she had in mind would challenge him to keep his cool. Mesmerized, he followed the path of her wet finger as she flicked each tight nipple. Then she stroked down her rib cage, over her flat belly and began circling her clit.

He stifled a groan as her hot channel tightened. "Keep that up and I'll come."

"I intend to keep it up. You won't come. I will."

"I wouldn't take bets on that, ma'am." He clenched his jaw but he couldn't make himself look away, even though watching her drove him crazy.

She gasped for air. "Hold on to me. I'm letting go of the post."

"Why?"

"To keep you…from coming." As she continued to touch herself, she slipped her thumb and forefinger around the base of his cock and squeezed.

He gulped at the sensation, which somehow lessened his urge to erupt. Then she loosened her grip and the pressure returned, taunting him with its power. Even though he hadn't moved at all, he was moments away from a climax. So was she. He could tell by her breathing and the faster motion of her finger.

When her first spasm hit, he thought he was a goner, until she squeezed him again, tighter this time. Her soft cry when she came was not much louder than a cricket's chirp. But ah, how her tremors surrounded and stroked every inch he'd buried deep inside her! It pushed the air from his lungs and made him shudder in reaction.

As her body quieted, she dragged in a breath and let go of his cock. "Your turn," she whispered.

Thank God for that. He figured he had about five seconds, tops. By now he couldn't tear his gaze away from the action as he pumped rapidly and his heart kept up a furious beat. The pace made her earrings tinkle like wind chimes. She was so wet, so hot, so…ready for another orgasm?

She drew in a sharp breath as if the sudden twinge had taken her by surprise.

He slowed and looked into her eyes, silently asking the question.

She shook her head. "Don't wait for me. I usually can't come in this position. That's why I…"

"I'm waiting." He didn't know how, but he'd do it and he'd give her a good ride in the process. Clamping down on the orgasm he'd expected to have very soon, he held her gaze and stroked more deliberately. "Maybe you should watch this time."

Her eyes widened.

"Go ahead. I dare you."

Grasping his shoulders, she looked down and her breath hitched.

Although he felt like thrusting fast and hard, he held back and created an easy motion that matched the rhythmic chirp of the crickets. "Like what you see?"

"Yeah."

He smiled at her breathless answer. "You know you're gonna come."

"Uh-huh."

He felt her heat up, felt the climax building, his and hers. Sex didn't always have to be wild and urgent. It could be like this—slow and rich, like warm syrup. There. Her fingers dug into his shoulders and she shuddered. Once more, maybe twice and she'd let go.

It only took once. When she came, her undulating channel and her muted wail of joy triggered his release. His breath hissed out between his teeth as he plunged deep, surrendering at last to wave upon wave of pleasure.

As he drifted in the aftermath of great sex, the creak of a door hinge penetrated his languid state.

"Dennis!" a woman called. "What are you doing out there?"

Grady put his mouth next to Sapphire's ear. "Stay very still."

She nodded.

"Thought I heard something," the guy named Dennis called back. "Don't want those skunks setting up house under the porch again. Think I'll look around."

From the corner of his eye, Grady saw the beam of a flashlight sweep the neighbor's yard. If Dennis decided to aim it in their direction, he'd discover two people locked together in an obviously sexual embrace. It was the risk they'd taken, after all.

"Sapphire and Amethyst's porch light is out," Dennis called to his wife. "Wonder if they know."

"You could go tell them, but the commercial's almost over. You'll miss the next part."

"I'll tell them tomorrow. Don't see anything out

here." He mounted the porch steps. The door hinge creaked again.

Sapphire started to giggle.

Grady wasn't sure how loud those giggles would get and so he disengaged himself from her, tossed the condom in the bushes and hustled them toward the front door.

Sure enough, her giggles got louder. "Did you just throw the condom in the bushes?"

"Shh. I'll get it in the morning."

"Okay. Sure." She was still laughing as they stumbled into the living room, both of their robes hanging half on and half off their bodies. "That was hysterical."

He grinned. "Glad you had fun."

"I had a blast. That position's always been a tricky one for orgasms."

"You weren't doing it with me."

"True." She gazed at him, a smile playing over her well-kissed mouth. "I think I hear your cat."

He had, too, and was trying to ignore the meowing. But in Gandalf's shoes, he wouldn't like being closed in a small space, either. "The tuna worked pretty well. Any left?"

"I only gave him half the can. He shouldn't have a steady diet of the stuff, but I can give him the other half to get him through the night."

"And us."

"Yep." She stifled a yawn.

"I saw that."

"Sorry. I didn't sleep well last night."

"Me, either. What do you say we feed the cat and turn in?"

"To sleep?"

He laughed. "Knowing this could damage my reputation as a stud, I'll admit that one more climax and I'll be done for the night."

"Your reputation is safe with me."

"Thanks." *But is my heart?* He wouldn't ask the question now, but soon. He was afraid she'd already stolen it when he wasn't looking.

9

Sapphire didn't normally sleep naked, but she did that night because a nightgown seemed silly when it would come off once Grady returned. He'd taken the rest of the tuna into the bathroom and was in there giving Gandalf his instructions, namely that the cat was to stay quiet the rest of the night. When he switched off the bathroom light and walked into the darkened bedroom, she was aroused in a lazy, relaxed way she'd never felt with other men.

The whisper of his footsteps on the carpet signaled her body to flush and moisten. The sound of his breathing caused her nipples to grow taut. The snap of latex sent a message to her core and the sweet ache returned. She was ready.

"Once more," he murmured as he climbed into bed and gathered her into his arms.

"Once more," she echoed, and opened her thighs.

"Nothing fancy." He entered her with one firm thrust. She sighed with pleasure. "I don't need fancy."

"We'll call it sleepy sex."

"Sleepy sex. I love it."

Leaning down, he kissed her gently. "I hope you do." And he began to move.

She knew him now—the friction of his cock, the rhythm of his strokes, the press of his fingers as he lifted her hips to drive deeper. Her body knew him, too, and her response came quickly. Wrapping her arms around his strong back, she arched upward with a moan as her orgasm flowed over her.

He pushed home once more and shuddered in her arms. "So good," he said, gasping for breath. "So damn good."

"Yeah." She hugged him close and smiled in the darkness. Sleepy sex. She was a fan.

He'd thought to bring in the wastebasket from the bathroom so he didn't have to leave the bed to dispose of the condom. That preplanning also made her smile. As she nestled against his muscled body and drifted off to sleep, she felt more content than she had in months, maybe years.

Sometime during the night she woke up still enclosed in his arms, her back against his warm chest and her bottom nudged against his currently inactive package. She lay there staring into the darkness, her contentment replaced with anxiety. What the hell was she doing inviting him to spend the week with her? Was she insane?

One night, considering the situation with Gandalf, was understandable. That would be resolved tomorrow, though. Gandalf was a temporary visitor and she'd never intended for the cat to occupy her bathroom for a week. He deserved more freedom than that.

Once the shelter vet gave him a clean bill of health, the Art Barn was a logical alternative for him until they knew whether he had a family in the area. He'd be fine in the office at night, especially if he was allowed to roam the entire barn during the day. He'd make friends with the artists. At the end of the week Grady could decide if he wanted to take Gandalf home to Cody.

That all made perfect sense, unlike asking Grady to leave Ben and Molly's guest room and move in with her. If that wasn't an invitation to begin a relationship, she didn't know what was. Great sex and a shared love of blueberry-cheesecake ice cream had addled her brain. It wasn't the first time that kind of thing had happened, but she liked to think she'd learned from her mistakes. Apparently not.

"What's up?" Grady's drowsy voice rumbled in her ear.

"Nothing. Go back to sleep."

"Can't. You're all tense."

"Sorry." She took a deep breath and started through one of her relaxation techniques.

"Is it a project? Sometimes I can't sleep if I'm thinking about a design."

Why did he have to be so considerate? It tempted her to think of him as an exception to the rule, but they were only a couple of days into this. Fatal flaws took weeks or months to show themselves.

She sighed. "It's not a project." *It's you.* But how could she admit all her misgivings after the fact? That was plain mean on a personal level. She also had an obligation to the shelter and her upcoming event. Causing problems with the star of the show wasn't a great way to proceed.

Besides, he'd done nothing to deserve that kind of rejection. *Yet.* Past experience told her that he would disillusion her sooner or later, and she'd rather skip that part, thank you very much. But if she said any of that now, she'd sound paranoid.

Gently, he urged her to turn toward him. "I've wanted to ask you this but I've put it off."

"Don't ask me." Panic constricted her chest. "Let's just go back to sleep."

"You're trembling like a leaf. What are you afraid of?"

"You!" She hadn't meant to say it but he'd pushed her.

"Me? I'm the biggest pussycat you'll ever meet!"

"Not you, exactly. Artists in general."

"Good grief." He chuckled. "We're the least scary group in the world. We make love, not war. You should know. You're one of us."

"Oh, Grady." She cradled his face, scruffy with the beard he'd shave off in the morning, probably with her razor. "Artists can make war, too, only they make war on the spirit. I've learned that the hard way, and I—"

"Hang on, Sapphire. Who are we talking about? If someone's been crushing your artistic spirit, I want names and locations. I'm a welder. I have muscle mass."

She smiled at that. She wanted him to be her defender, her knight in shining armor, but others had claimed that position and shown themselves to be unworthy. She'd lost the ability to believe in knights and flashing swords.

Drawing in a breath, she took stock. She'd started the conversation and she couldn't leave it dangling. Besides, they were supposed to go to dinner at her parents' house and all sorts of personal info could pop up during that encounter. "I have a weakness for creative guys."

He caught her hands and nibbled on her fingers. "My good luck."

"The first one was Gregory. I fell madly in love with him when we were in high school. He turned out to be gay."

"Sapphire, I'm so sorry, but obviously, I don't have that issue."

"Then there was Jeremy, who seemed to mean well and was insanely talented but *so* undependable. He couldn't remember appointments, my birthday or when the rent was due. He was more child than man. Living with him was exhausting and I ended up caretaking instead of doing my work. He cried when I broke up with him and I felt awful, but he wasn't an adult."

"You don't need someone like that."

"I figured that out and moved on to Edgar, also a talented artist. Neat and focused. But ultimately, so jealous of my talent that he started undermining me and came damn near to destroying my confidence."

"Dear God." Grady stroked her hair. "That's criminal. Where is he now? I'd be happy to rearrange his face for you."

"I don't know and I wouldn't tell you if I did. I don't want you arrested for assaulting someone who's not worth it."

His voice was low and dangerous. "I could be in and out without leaving a trace. Thunder Mountain boys know things."

"I still wouldn't tell you where he is." But it worried her that he cared that much. She didn't want him to become invested.

"I could ask Rosie. She knows every blessed thing that goes on in this town."

"Don't ask her. I decided long ago to let sleeping dogs lie."

He combed her hair away from her face. "Is that it, then? Your collection of slimy artists?"

"One more. Cal. Women loved him. I loved him. I didn't figure out until months into the relationship that he was sleeping with every attractive woman who gave him a second glance. When I confronted him, he claimed that such behavior fueled his creativity. He said artists couldn't be held to the same conventional standard as other people."

"That's bullshit."

She sighed. "I know, but Cal was the final straw."

He didn't say anything for a while. When he finally spoke, his tone was wary. "So what's this all about, then?"

"This?"

"You, me, getting naked. *This*."

"We're attracted to each other."

"Yeah, and?"

"At first I decided not to give in to that attraction, but…"

"But you did." He reached over and switched on the bedside lamp. "Even though Cal was the final straw." He turned back to her, a question in his brown eyes. "Does that mean you're reevaluating?"

Her stomach hurt. She couldn't lie to him, but because he'd asked the question, he probably wouldn't like the answer.

His expression closed down. "You're not reevaluating."

"No." She swallowed. "I just—"

"Wanted some good sex." He turned away and swung his legs over the edge of the bed.

"Didn't you?"

"You know I did. But I didn't realize my days were numbered." He stood and pulled on the robe.

"Grady, we don't even live in the same town."

He pulled the robe across his chest as best he could and tied the sash with an angry jerk of his wrist. "And that's an issue we'd have to deal with. Maybe we're not destined to have more than a few nights of wild sex. But it never occurred to me that you'd already decided that's all we'd have. Now I know." He started for the door.

"Where are you going?"

"To eat ice cream. Double-chocolate fudge brownie is my second favorite." He left the room.

Flopping back on the pillow, she stared at the ceiling. She'd certainly made a mess of that, hadn't she? She could have kept her big mouth shut and they'd still be cuddled in this bed.

But now she knew something more about him, too. While she'd ruled out getting seriously involved, he hadn't. He'd thought that was a possibility, even if it might be a remote one. He hadn't seen their geographic distance as being an insurmountable barrier. If they'd continued to get along this week, they would have had this confrontation eventually.

The freezer door opened and then the silverware drawer rattled. He must have the ice cream and a spoon. By now it was too cold to sit out on the porch. The scrape of a chair told her he'd stayed at the kitchen table. She didn't like to think of him in there brooding.

She climbed out of bed and put on her robe. She'd wounded him, and even though that had never been her goal, she needed to say she was sorry.

He glanced up when she walked into the kitchen. "Hey."

"Hey, yourself." She couldn't read his expression, which was probably his intent. She got a spoon out of the drawer and sat across from him. "Can I have a bite?"

"You bet. Your ice cream." He shoved the carton across the table.

"Thanks." She took a spoonful and pushed it back over.

He sent it sailing back. "You keep it for a while. I ate too fast. Brain freeze."

She probably shouldn't laugh at a time like this, but it was funny.

"I know, right?" He rubbed his bristly chin. "I've been eating ice cream by myself since I was two. You'd think I'd have the hang of it by now."

"Maybe you wanted to freeze your brain for a while."

"Maybe."

"Grady, I'm really sorry if I misled you. I didn't mean to." She did her best not to stare at him but he was extremely stare-worthy, with his tousled hair, roguish beard and the swath of muscled chest the robe couldn't cover.

"See, the way you're looking at me right now is part of the problem. That look gets me hot."

"Sorry." She dropped her gaze from the hunk across the table to the hunks of chocolate in the ice cream.

"But the thing is, I like getting hot when there's a chance I can do something about it."

She glanced up. "Oh?"

"Could be that brain freeze helps a person think better, because I've been doing some of that." He blew out a breath. "I have to take some responsibility for the situation. You gave me no reason to think you wanted more than sex from me. Just the opposite. I could tell you wanted to avoid anything mushy."

"Which sounds pretty coldhearted, like all that interests me is your package and I don't care about you as a person."

"I know that's not true." He smiled. "And it's okay to be enamored of my cock, just like it's okay for you to look at me as if you need it right this minute."

Heat spiraled down between her thighs and she was ready again.

Resting his corded arms on the table, he leaned forward, a gleam in his brown eyes. "Do you need it right this minute, Sapphire?"

Her heart pounded loud enough that he could probably hear the staccato beat. She nodded.

"As it happens, I'm prepared for that contingency." He pulled a condom out of his pocket and pushed away from the table. "Come on over here, sweet lady. Let's try that position again, the one where you think it's difficult for you to come."

Trembling with need, she left her chair and walked around the table. There was nothing atmospheric or subtle this time. The overhead light was on, leaving nothing to the imagination.

Hooking a finger in her sash, he pulled it open. "You're shaking."

"Uh-huh."

"Scared?"

"No."

"Good, because you never have to be afraid of me." Spanning her waist with both hands, he hoisted her to the edge of the table. "I'll never hurt you."

"I know."

"No, you don't. But that's okay. I'll make a believer of you." He moved between her spread thighs. "To start with, I'm not going to kiss you, because I'd give you whisker burn."

She smoothed a hand over his beard. "I don't care."

"I do. Now grab on to my shoulders, because I'm coming in." Holding her gaze, he slid slowly forward. "You're very wet."

"Mmm." She couldn't talk. She was too busy absorbing this moment when he filled her and locked himself in tight. His eyes had darkened to the color of rich chocolate.

"That'll make it even easier. We're gonna tilt back a little." Holding her hips, he leaned toward her. "Wrap your legs around me. Perfect. Now hang on." He began to thrust, easily at first, then faster and faster yet.

The intense friction made her gasp and within seconds it made her come. Her cries echoed off the hard surfaces as he kept pumping at that same rapid speed. She came again, and this time so did he. Bellowing at the top of his lungs, he closed his eyes and drove in tight. The strong pulse of his cock blended with the ripples of her climax to create the most dramatic orgasm she'd ever had.

Slowly, he opened his eyes and grinned. "Now, that's what I call a good time."

Unexpected tears pricked her eyelids. "Thank you."

"You're welcome. You got something in your eyes? They're watering."

She sniffed. "Must be dust. I'm fine. But I wasn't thanking you for the sex, which was amazing. I was thanking you because you've forgiven me."

"Nothing to forgive. I was missing some critical info and made a wrong assumption. Now I get it and we're good."

She wasn't sure what that meant but she wasn't going to ask him to clarify. "We should go back to bed." She glanced at the kitchen clock. "It's past three."

"And I just heard Gandalf. I probably woke him up when I yelled."

She smiled. "I liked it when you yelled. Very manly."

"Except now we have a crying cat." He eased away from her and disposed of the condom in the kitchen trash. "I'd better go in there and settle him down." He tied his robe and had started out of the kitchen when he turned back. "I didn't put away the—"

"Never mind. I'll do it. Go see your cat."

"Meet you in bed."

"Okay." After he left, she picked up the ice-cream carton. He'd loved her so fast and so well that the ice cream hadn't had time to melt much. She put the lid back on and tucked it in the freezer.

She'd never known a man like Grady. When he was upset, he didn't shout or bang around or sulk. Instead he ate ice cream and thought about things. He'd promised never to hurt her. He'd also vowed that eventually she'd believe in him.

They were beautiful words and she'd certainly heard beautiful words before. Creative men were usually good with them. Was she wrong to think Grady was different? Probably. She'd been wrong before. But for now, the storm had passed. He appeared willing to enjoy what they had for the time they had it. That made her happy.

10

GRADY SLEPT LIKE the dead until Sapphire's alarm went off at six. She reached over and shut it off. Then she lay very still, breathing lightly. He was about to find out if she was a morning person.

He hoped so, and not because he had the woody of the century. If he and Sapphire expected to get showered and out the door with Gandalf in tow before seven, they'd have to move it, and soon.

His interest in her attitude toward mornings went beyond whether she enjoyed sex at sunrise. He loved mornings. If she didn't and they worked through all the other crap she'd thrown at him last night, they'd still have that minor issue of different body clocks.

His last girlfriend had hated mornings with a passion. It hadn't been the only reason they'd broken up, but it had been a factor. He was already half in love with Sapphire, though, and a body-clock misalignment wouldn't change that. Nothing would change that after she'd taken the initiative to come into the kitchen and smooth things over.

They'd been well and truly smoothed. He'd accept part of the blame for the blow to his ego. He'd sensed something had her spooked and now he knew what it was. Her past experience had taught her not to trust any man who created things for a living.

He even understood her attitude. That didn't mean he believed that she was only in it for the sex. Maybe she was now, but she wouldn't be for long if he had anything to say about it.

"Grady?" Her voice was thick with sleep.

"What?"

"We should get up."

"I know." Maybe *not* a morning person. Oh, well.

"But I have a problem."

"You don't want to get up?"

"That's not the problem. I woke up from a dream of having sex with you and it left me sort of…achy. I was wondering if—"

"Say no more." He reached for the box of condoms. "I've got you covered." He didn't linger over the niceties. This morning his beard would scrape the rust off a tailpipe. But his cock was easily as hard as one when he sank into her slick channel.

She hadn't been kidding. That must have been some dream. A few quick strokes and she orgasmed, which allowed him to do the same. Breathing hard, he pushed the damp hair back from her face. "There you go."

"Thanks." She smiled up at him. "Good morning."

"And so it is." He kissed her lightly without making contact with his beard. "I'm using your razor, if that's okay."

"Go ahead. Take whatever you need. I'll go upstairs to shower and meet you in the kitchen. I have some yogurt in the fridge, so help yourself. We'll get coffee at the barn."

"What about tuna?"

"I have a couple more cans in the pantry. Can opener is on the counter. He'll get dry food later at the barn."

"Got it." They each left the bed without any more conversation. She didn't put on a robe and neither did he.

She grabbed some undies from the dresser and clothes from the closet before hurrying upstairs. Because he was a guy, he watched her running around the room naked and was so glad they'd had a quickie before starting the day.

Once she left, he tossed the robes over a chair and pulled up the covers on the bed. No sense making it when they'd be rolling around in it again tonight. For a little while last night, that had been in doubt, but a woman didn't wake up and ask for sex if she intended to send a guy packing. At least, this one wouldn't.

In the kitchen, he located the tuna, opened a can and found a bowl like the one she'd used for the first batch. When she'd first explained her problem with artists as partners and he'd gone off to the kitchen to lick his wounds and eat ice cream, he'd considered setting up sleeping quarters in the barn. What a stupid move that would have been.

His younger self would have done something like that to make a point. Thank God he'd reconsidered as he'd spooned in the ice cream and given himself brain freeze. He wasn't like those guys who'd treated her so rotten, but going off to sulk every night in the Art Barn might convince her that he was exactly like them.

When she'd walked into the kitchen and grabbed a spoon, that gesture had helped get his head on straight, too. She liked him. She craved his body. Maybe she'd lumped him in with those other schmucks, but he could fix that. At least, he could if he didn't create a rift between them by reacting like an asshole.

Then he'd caught her looking at him as if she'd gone a week without candy and his dick was made of caramel. Only an idiot would turn away from that. He wasn't always as smart as he should be, but he'd figured that out real quick.

She wanted him, but she didn't trust him or herself. Given her history, that wasn't surprising. He had a week to show her that he wasn't cut from the same cloth, that he wasn't gay, juvenile, a jealous bastard or a cheating one. A week wasn't much time, but it was what he had.

Gandalf was overjoyed to see him. The cat seemed more excited about Grady's presence than the tuna, which was touching. So Grady stroked him and encouraged him to eat. Once he'd buried his nose in the bowl, Grady turned on the shower and hopped in.

A thump a few seconds later told him Gandalf was showering with him yet again. He turned to look at the cat. "That's unnatural. You're not supposed to do that."

Gandalf regarded him steadily.

"No, really. Cats don't like water. Didn't you get the memo?"

Ignoring the shower pelting down on him, Gandalf walked over and started licking Grady's leg.

Laughing, Grady finished his shower quickly. Once again he had to towel off the cat and himself. He piled the towels in a corner because everything would have to be washed. While he tackled his beard with Sapphire's pink razor, Gandalf hopped up on the sink, sat down and started purring.

"I'm getting kinda attached to you, cat." He met Gandalf's blue-eyed gaze in the mirror. "Liam's moving out as soon as he renovates that house and marries Hope. I could use some company. What do you say?"

Gandalf made the half-purr, half-meow noise that was definitely a response to the question.

"I'll consider that a yes. But first I have to make sure I'm not taking you away from some family who loves you. If we can't locate anybody in a week, you can hit the road with me, buddy. Sound good?"

The cat's sharp meow made him grin. "Hey, I'm excited about the idea, too. It's a deal." He finished up with the razor. It wasn't the closest shave he'd ever had, but at least he no longer looked like a vagrant. "Stay put for a bit, okay? I'll be back to get you." He left, closing the cat in. Gandalf heartily protested. "I know. I promise you won't have to stay there all day."

Not long afterward, dressed and fueled up with raspberry yogurt, he came back to the bathroom and scooped the cat into his arms. They were even slightly ahead of schedule, so he'd had time to go out front and retrieve the condom he'd thrown in the bushes.

Sapphire had loaned him a blue buffalo-plaid shirt that was way too big to have been hers. But Gandalf had spent the night lying on his shirt, and wearing it would spread hair all over the house. This one likely had belonged to one of the scumbags she'd told him about. He wore it, but he'd change at his first opportunity. He didn't want her associating him with that bunch.

Gandalf began to shake when Grady climbed into the passenger seat of Sapphire's purple truck. "He's scared."

"I'm not surprised." Sapphire started the engine. "He doesn't know what's going to happen to him." She looked over at Gandalf. "It'll be okay, kitty. You're safe with us."

Grady liked the way she'd said that—*safe with us*—

like they were Team Gandalf. In a way they were. They'd worked together on this deal, although she had the resources and he'd simply been the support staff. "Do you have a plan for this guy?"

"A potential plan." She backed the truck out of the drive. "See what you think. We'll close him in the office and give him some dry food while we take care of the ferals. Then we'll take him over to the shelter for a quick vet check. Assuming he's fine, I'll contact the co-op members to see if they're okay with him staying at the barn while we put the word out and see if he belongs anywhere."

"Think they'll be okay with that?"

"I'm sure they will since we've talked about having a barn cat eventually, but I want to ask first."

"And if no one shows up to claim him?" He suddenly realized she might assume Gandalf would become a permanent fixture at the Art Barn. He wouldn't blame her if she wanted to keep him. He was a great cat.

She glanced at him with a smile in her eyes. "You get first dibs."

"Thanks." He blew out a breath. "Selfishly, I hope no one claims him." He stroked Gandalf's soft coat. Thanks to a couple of showers, it was looking pretty good.

"I doubt they will. I think you have yourself a cat."

"Then I need to get him some stuff today. A brush, for one thing. And his own food and water dish. And a litter box and bed. I guess if he's going to stay in the barn this week, he'll be there by himself at night." Grady scratched behind the cat's ears and murmured whatever soothing things came into his head. He wasn't crazy about leaving the cat alone in the barn all through the night but he also wanted to be with Sapphire. He finally came up with a compromise. "How about if I work on Rosie's sculpture for a while tonight?"

"Do you want to cancel going over to my mom and dad's for dinner?"

"I forgot about that. No, I want to go. I could come here afterward, though."

She gave him a knowing look. "I'm sure Gandalf would be appreciative."

"I'll lose some time today buying his stuff and picking up my clothes from Ben and Molly's, so working tonight could make that up. Which reminds me, do you think he'll be all right while I run those errands?"

Her lips twitched as if she wanted to laugh. "Grady, he'll be *fine*. If you're like this with a cat, Lord help you if you have a kid."

"Am I being overprotective?"

"Just a little. It's cute, actually."

"Ugh." He scowled at the cat. "Gandalf, you're gonna have to man up, because I won't be coddling you anymore, buddy. I can't have the lady calling me *cute*. I'm looking for descriptions like *hot*, *ripped* and *sexy as hell*."

She lost it. As her laughter spilled out, he got a kick out of her pink cheeks and sparkling eyes. Her outfit sparkled today, too. Her blouse and skirt were dotted with sequins and her long earrings glittered with multicolored crystals that drew his attention to her graceful neck.

Good thing he had an armful of cat or he'd be tempted to lean over and kiss her there. "Damn, but you're beautiful, Sapphire."

Her breath caught. "Thank you." She looked over at him and for a brief moment soft yearning filled her eyes.

She wants to believe I mean it. That I'm not some

selfish bastard who says things like that and then acts like a jerk.

Then her expression changed and a teasing light replaced the glow that had been there. She returned her attention to the road. "You're not so bad yourself."

He could guess what was coming next.

"I'd go so far as to say you're hot, ripped and sexy as hell."

"You're welcome to come up with your own words. Those were just suggestions to start you off."

"All right." She drummed her fingers on the steering wheel. "Ogle-worthy and lickable eye candy."

"Not bad."

"An orgasmic fantasy, a walking wet dream, a—"

"That'll do. You're making Gandalf uncomfortable."

"He understands English?"

"No, but he's sitting on my lap."

"Oh." She smirked. "I see."

"Fortunately, you can't see, because the cat's hiding the evidence." As they approached the Art Barn, he noticed a tan pickup parked beside his truck. "So who's here?"

"That belongs to George Reavis. He's our woodcarver. He didn't make it over yesterday because he and his wife took a quick trip to see the grandkids. Now that George is here, we should have the whole contingent today." She opened her door. "You coming in?"

"Go ahead. Gandalf and I will be along shortly, after decompression happens."

She looked contrite. "Sorry."

"Hey, don't ever be sorry that you got a rise out of me. You're a lusty lady and I treasure that. I plan to treasure it even more tonight."

"Good."

"It will be. Now head on in and start on the food bowls."

"Okay." Bending down, she dipped her head under the brim of his hat and kissed him lightly on the mouth. Then she drew back and smiled. "See you in a minute."

He would have pulled her close for a more satisfying kiss but couldn't risk letting go of the cat. He settled for a mild protest. "You can do better than that."

"I didn't want to make things worse."

"A little bit of tongue never hurt anybody."

"You're a scoundrel, Grady Magee." Pushing his hat up and cupping the back of his head, she angled her mouth over his and thrust her tongue inside.

Then she proceeded to kiss the living daylights out of him. It was all he could do to stay calm and hold on to Gandalf without squeezing the poor animal.

After sweetly torturing him for a good long while, she finally lifted her mouth away. "Did you like that better?"

"Much." He dragged in air.

"How's your lap?"

"Painful, but I'm not gonna mention it."

Leaning back, she gazed at him. "Better not. Hang on. You're wearing my lipstick." She grabbed her purse from behind her seat, then dug out a tissue and wiped his mouth. After settling his hat where it belonged, she peeked in the rearview mirror and wiped her mouth, too. "That needs a do-over."

By the time she'd reapplied her lipstick, he'd recovered enough to leave the truck. "Crisis is over. I can walk in with you now."

"Then I'll get your door." She came around to the passenger side and helped him out.

Happily, Gandalf didn't sink his claws into the plaid

shirt when Grady stepped down to the pavement. Maybe the cat recognized the place and wasn't too worried about going inside.

"So give me some background on George," Grady said as they neared the building. "I'm trying to keep everybody straight."

"He's retired military, about sixty, has a bushy white beard, a great laugh and a little potbelly."

"You just described Santa Claus."

"He used to have a gig as Santa but now he only dresses up for our holiday events at the barn. I've known him for about five years. We did craft shows together and that's when we came up with the idea for the co-op."

"His carving's really nice. I was thinking of getting something for my mom, maybe the heron. She loves waterbirds."

"I'm sure he'd be honored." She held the door open for him. "We're still ahead of schedule. Let's close Gandalf in the office with a bowl of dry food and go say hello to George before we feed the ferals. I know he's eager to meet you."

"Sounds great."

Moments later Gandalf was munching away and didn't even look up when Grady and Sapphire slipped out, closing the office door behind them.

"He might just be happy to be out of the bathroom," Grady said as they walked down the barn aisle to George's spot.

"I hear the *trip-trap* of feet!" boomed a voice from the last stall on the left, right across from Grady's.

"I'm bringing you a visitor," Sapphire called back.

A Santa look-alike appeared in the aisle holding a knife and a piece of wood. He even wore the frameless half-glasses Santa favored. "I'm gonna take a wild guess that this is Grady Magee."

"In the flesh." Grady stepped forward and offered his hand. "I admire your work."

"And I yours." He transferred the knife to his shirt pocket and shook Grady's hand. "Thanks for coming up to our event! I'm a huge fan. So's my wife, Eloise. We have one of your smaller pieces in our living room."

"That's great to hear. Thank you." Grady smiled. "I've been thinking about your heron for my mother. She'd love it."

"Good eye, son. That heron was a bitch to carve, but I'm mighty proud of it. I took a peek at what you're working on. Wolves, right?"

"It's for Rosie, his foster mom," Sapphire said. "It's a surprise, so we're all sworn to secrecy."

"I won't tell. Rosie and Herb are good people. A credit to the community."

"I'll go along with that." Grady rolled his shoulders. The stupid shirt had begun to itch. It hadn't before, so he thought it might be all in his head, but he wanted it off. "Listen, I need to run a quick errand, so I'll leave you two and be back in a little while. Great meeting you, George. And if you'd set that heron aside for me, I'd be obliged."

"I'll put a sold sign on it right now. See you soon. I look forward to sharing the workspace with you."

"Same here."

Sapphire glanced at him. "I'll walk you out."

"No need." He gave her a quick smile. "I'll be back before you know it." It was just a dumb shirt, but it was bugging the hell out of him. He moved swiftly toward the front door.

Sapphire kept up. "You're acting twitchy. What's up?"

"I have to pick up my stuff from Ben and Molly's sometime, so I might as well do it now. Then that part will be taken care of. And I can return this shirt to you."

She followed him out the door. "No rush on that."

"Yeah, there is. Whose was it?"

"Does it matter?"

"Just morbid curiosity."

"Jeremy's."

When he reached his truck, he turned to face her. "Jeremy was the immature slob, right?"

"Right."

"And you dumped him, so the shirt means nothing." Or so he tried to tell himself.

She took a deep breath. "That's not quite true."

Oh, God. She still loved him.

"There's a reason I kept the shirt, which he forgot that he left at my place. So typical."

"What reason?" He braced himself for a sob story about how Jeremy was bad for her but she couldn't forget him and she slept in his shirt every night except this last one when they'd boinked each other senseless.

"I keep it to remind myself never to get involved with someone like him again."

He was somewhat relieved but still not in a happy place. "So now I'm wearing this negative reminder."

"It really was the only thing in the house that would fit you! I worried about offering it but thought it would only be temporary. I wasn't ever going to tell you where it had come from."

"Have you kept anything else? From the other guys?"

She hesitated.

"Never mind. It's none of my business."

"Yeah, it is, now that I loaned you the shirt. I just— Nobody knows I've kept reminders, not even Amethyst.

It's my own silly way of trying to stay on track. I didn't keep anything from Gregory. He was trying to deny he was gay, poor guy. That was biology, not a character flaw. I started keeping reminders when Jeremy left his shirt."

"And the next guy?"

"Edgar was a wine snob and made fun of people who didn't drink the best, like me, for example. He left a bottle of wine worth about two hundred bucks. I've never opened it but I keep it so I can remember what arrogance looks like."

"What about the cheater?"

"I kept the sentimental card he sent with his Valentine's Day roses. The woman who works at the floral shop is a friend from high school. We went out for drinks one night and after a few too many she told me he'd sent the same message and bouquet to three girlfriends that day."

The shirt itched even worse now. "Then you need this back." He took off his hat and laid it on the fender of his truck. After undoing a couple of buttons, he pulled it over his head and gave it to her. The morning breeze was chilly but he'd never been so glad to get rid of a piece of clothing in his life.

"Grady, I apologize for the shirt."

He shrugged. "Like you said, I needed something and this was what you had." He gazed at her. "Sounds like you've put a lot of effort into deciding what you don't want."

"I suppose."

"Have you put any thought into what you do want?"

She seemed taken aback by the question.

"It's another way to approach the problem." Grabbing her by the shoulders, he gave her a quick kiss. Then he put on his hat and unlocked his truck. When he drove away, she was standing in the same spot staring after him, exactly as she'd done three weeks ago.

He might be tempting fate to make a prediction, but she'd confided some important information in the past twelve hours. He might be ahead of where he'd been three weeks ago.

_11_

SAPPHIRE HAD PLENTY to think about as she maneuvered through her day. Fortunately, George was in charge of handling any customers who came in, which left her free to go with Grady to the shelter for Gandalf's vet check. The cat got a perfect bill of health and the shelter set their pet alert program in motion. If anyone in the general area had reported losing a gray long-haired male, the shelter would hear about it.

She'd texted all the co-op members and they were fine with having Gandalf as a guest for the next week. She'd warned them that he likely wouldn't be permanent. But a barn cat was still a good idea and she hoped eventually Fred would be socialized enough to take on the job.

Grady had fetched his things and was dressed in a faded blue Western shirt instead of the buffalo-plaid one that had caused so much trouble. She'd known that loaning it to him was a mistake. She hadn't wanted to be reminded of Jeremy when she looked at Grady any more than he'd wanted to serve as a reminder.

He had a sixth sense about things. She'd counted on him wearing it for a couple of hours until he'd picked up his clothes. Turned out a couple of hours had been a long enough time to create a problem.

Then again, that tense conversation might have been necessary. He'd made an excellent point. In her determination not to repeat the same pattern, she'd focused only on the negatives she was avoiding. She hadn't thought at all about the positives she was seeking.

That was tricky because her previous lovers had possessed good qualities, too, ones that had attracted her in the first place. She'd conveniently pushed away thoughts about those because, hey, when a girl broke up with someone, she wanted to think of him as totally evil, right?

Creativity was the real bugaboo for her, the one that set off warning bells. Jeremy had been creative but irresponsible. Edgar had been creative but arrogant. Cal had been creative but fickle. The one trait they had in common, the behavior that drew her like a bee to pollen, was their ability to enrich the world with their art.

Maybe she hadn't focused on what she wanted because she knew subconsciously that she still craved a man with that magical gift, required it, in fact, before he was interesting to her. In her experience, imagination had always been linked to a fatal flaw. She hadn't discovered Grady's, but she had to believe he had one. It just hadn't shown itself yet.

Whatever her personal misgivings might be about him, the co-op members obviously loved having him around. Inspiration hummed through the building. Usually, the artists wandered around chatting with each other and generally wasting time, but today there had been none of that. At the end of the day when they gathered in the office for a last cup of coffee and the cookies Arlene had brought, everyone thanked Grady for energizing them with his work ethic.

Grady shrugged and looked mildly embarrassed by the praise. "Just trying to set a good example for the cat."

"I believe it," George said. "Gandalf kept an eagle eye on you all afternoon from the top of that cat tree."

"Yeah, that was a great purchase." Sapphire had been a little startled when Grady had gone for cat-care essentials and had come back with a six-foot multitiered playground for Gandalf in addition to the smaller items.

Occupying a far corner of Grady's work area, it allowed Gandalf to observe his hero without being anywhere near the torch. He was wary of the instrument but clearly wanted to keep Grady in sight. The carpeted structure let him do that.

"Now's a good time to vote on how we handle having a cat here at night," Sapphire said. "We can give him the run of the place or close him in the office."

"I vote we give him the run of the place." George grabbed another cookie. "We all store our supplies when we go home, so there's not much he could get into and I'll bet he'd rather be free than cooped up."

"I feel the same." Arlene reached down and petted Gandalf, who'd followed everyone into the office. "He's a good cat. Let him roam." She glanced around. "Everybody agree?" They all did.

"That's settled, then. " Sapphire drained her coffee cup. "I need to load up the food dishes for the ferals. Any questions about the event? We're only three days away, so now's the time to talk about anything we've forgotten."

"Now that I think about it," Grady said, "we should close Gandalf in the office during the event. He might be okay with the crowd, but I don't want to take a chance he'd get spooked and run off."

"Good call," George said. "For one thing, we'll have little kids here. We don't know how he'd react to them."

"Then we'll make sure he's tucked away before we open the doors. Anything else?" When nobody spoke, she gave a quick little nod. "Okay, then. See you all tomorrow."

Everyone left but Grady. She glanced at him, not quite sure where they stood. They'd had very few moments alone today and he hadn't used any of those moments to talk about this morning's incident. "Want to help me feed?"

"I do." Laying his hat on the counter, he moved in close and rested his hands on her shoulders. "But I desperately need a kiss." He massaged her shoulders gently. "Think that could be arranged?"

"Absolutely." Her pulse quickened as it always did the minute he put those talented hands on her. So he was ready to continue what they'd started. Hallelujah. She wound her arms around his neck. "But the cats are out there waiting and we're due at my parents' in an hour."

"And I need a shower and a change of clothes, so I'll make it quick." His mouth hovered over hers. "Semiquick." He touched down and lightly tasted her lips. Then with a low moan, he gripped her shoulders and delved deep. The erotic movement of his tongue told her what he really wanted.

So did she. Tunneling her fingers through his hair, she whimpered and tried to wiggle closer, but he held her fast, keeping their bodies apart.

Gasping, he lifted his head. "If I let myself settle against your hot body, guaranteed we'll do more than kiss and we don't have time."

"Are you saying you brought—"

"I told you I'd always be prepared." He pressed kisses at the corners of her mouth. "Which means I have a condom in my pocket, but we're not gonna use it."

She gulped for air. "No, we're not."

"No matter how much my cock aches for you."

"I ache for you, too."

"That helps." His chuckle sounded strained. "Sort of. No, it doesn't. God, how I want to—" A sharp, demanding meow stopped him in midsentence.

They both glanced down.

Gandalf sat primly, front paws together and fluffy tail wrapped around his feet. He stared up at them with his sky blue eyes, blinked once and uttered the same quick meow.

"Oh, boy." Sapphire couldn't help laughing. "I don't know if you got that, but the message is clear to me."

"He's hungry?"

"I doubt it. Last time I checked, he had dry food in his dish. I'm guessing he wants you to quit fooling around with me and pay attention to him."

"Really?"

"Really. They get jealous, too, you know." She'd meant it as kind of a joke, but his expression told her he hadn't taken it that way. Whoops.

"Sapphire, I wasn't jealous." Then he blew out a breath. "No, that's a damn lie. I didn't like thinking you'd kept an old boyfriend's shirt. If I'm being totally honest, I still don't like it, even though it's supposed to be there as a warning. It's like *he's* there, and worse yet, he's one of the reasons you're afraid to get close to me."

She swallowed. "Yes, he is."

"That's not fair, you know, to judge me based on what another guy—"

"Three other guys."

"I don't care if it was twenty." His gaze intensified. "I'm me, an individual, yet you've lumped me in with them and I don't like it."

"I don't blame you."

Gandalf meowed again, but this time more plaintively.

With a heavy sigh, Grady rubbed the back of his neck. "You know what? We need to feed those cats."

"I do, but you don't have to. I'll give you my house key. You can go back and take your time cleaning up."

"Think we need a breather?"

"Maybe."

"First I'll give Gandalf a nice brushing. Then I'll take you up on that offer. Come on, cat. I left your brush in your tree house." He started out of the kitchen and Gandalf trotted after him, tail in the air like a victory flag.

"I'll leave my key on the desk in the office."

He kept walking. "Thanks," he called over his shoulder. "See you soon."

Although she felt icky and disoriented by the exchange, she forced herself to get out the bowls, fill them quickly and layer them into the basket. She pulled her keys from her purse on the kitchen counter, then unhooked the one for the front door and laid it on the desk as she went through the office.

Fred was there with the other cats when she set out the bowls. After last night's episode, he didn't want to show up late. Apparently, he hadn't appreciated waiting for his food and was determined to claim a bowl before another cat edged him out again.

All eleven looked healthy. She always eyeballed each one during feeding time to make sure some issue hadn't cropped up, but they moved well and ate with enthusiasm. She hadn't fed them alone since Grady had arrived two nights ago. Funny how quickly she'd become used to having him there. The sound of his truck leaving the parking lot added to her funky mood.

Although they hadn't exactly fought, the spontaneous joy they'd first enjoyed might be gone temporarily— or maybe for good. He could always decide she wasn't worth the angst and back off completely but he probably wouldn't. The sex was too good. In spite of everything, she couldn't wait to be alone with him again and she knew he felt the same way.

Seeing her folks' reaction to him would be interesting. Her dad tended to like everyone, but her mom was pickier. Gregory had been the only boyfriend of hers she'd warmed to. When he'd finally accepted that he was gay, she'd been as supportive as his own folks had been. But her mom had never quite accepted any of the three guys who'd come along after Gregory.

Sapphire had become so absorbed in her thoughts that she hadn't noticed that the cats had begun to leave. It seemed nobody craved attention tonight. By the time she became aware, they were all headed back for the woods…all except Fred. He'd finished all the food in his bowl and he crouched there staring at her.

"Hey, Fred," she said softly. "How's it going?" Then she used a technique one of the shelter volunteers had taught her. She blinked. That was supposed to indicate friendly intentions. "You're a handsome boy, Freddie." She blinked again.

The cat blinked back.

She gave a slight gasp. "Oh, Fred, it makes me very happy that we exchanged blinks." She tried it again but an owl hooted nearby.

Fred tensed. Then he turned and bounded back to the shelter of the woods.

"That's okay, Freddie. You need to protect yourself against owls. Just not against me." Feeling triumphant, she collected the bowls and hurried into the barn. In the midst of washing them, she heard a cat purring. Sure enough, Gandalf had heard her come in and had decided to join her.

"I hate to tell you this, cat, but Grady's not with me." She finished cleaning the bowls and dried her hands. "But he plans to come back to see you later tonight." Crouching down, she held out her hand.

Gandalf came over and gave her a good sniff before bumping his head against her hand in an obvious bid to be petted.

She obliged him. "Any port in a storm, huh, Gandalf? Listen, kitty, I'd love to stay here and love on you, but I have places to go and people to see." After one last scratch, she stood.

The cat meowed in protest.

At least, that was what it sounded like to her. "Yeah, well, that's life, kiddo. Sometimes you're rolling in clover and sometimes you're wallowing in muck. Considering the fact that you've captured Grady's heart, I'd put you in the clover category." She picked up her purse and headed to the door. Gandalf followed her, so she exited quickly so he wouldn't dash out.

On the drive to her house she glanced at the dashboard clock. Running late. Locating her phone in her purse, she pulled it out and called her mom. "Hey, Grady and I are about fifteen minutes behind schedule."

Her mom laughed. "So he said when he called."

"He called you?"

"Not long ago. Must have found our number somewhere in your house. He said you were out feeding the cats and would need a little time to get cleaned up before you two came over. Is that code for having a quickie?"

"Mom!"

"Whether it is or not, I appreciate his call. He sounds nice on the phone."

"He is nice, but that doesn't change the fact that he's an artist."

"Has it occurred to you that your father and I are both artists?"

"I, um— Well, sure you are, but—"

"In case you haven't noticed, we've managed to stumble through twenty-nine years of marriage without killing each other. If artists are incapable of having a decent relationship, how do you explain that?"

The conversation was giving her a headache. "You're both obviously exceptions to the rule. I just pulled into the driveway, so I need to go. See you soon!"

"Don't rush, dear. I remember when your father and I started dating and we couldn't get enough of—"

"Bye, Mom." She so didn't want to hear whatever her mother had been about to confide. That topic hadn't been discussed when she'd dated Jeremy, Edgar or Cal. Why now? Had Grady won her over with a single phone call?

When she walked into the house, Grady was sitting there in the robe she'd loaned him. "I thought you'd be dressed."

"I bought us a little time for makeup sex."

"Makeup sex?" She put her purse on the table by the door. "We didn't have a fight."

He stood and came toward her. "No, but I said some things I shouldn't have. You have a right to handle your life however you want and I was out of line to suggest any different."

"And you have a right to be jealous and upset because you ended up wearing an old boyfriend's shirt this morning. I don't blame you in the least. That can't be pleasant, especially for someone with your level of testosterone."

Stopping in his tracks, he stared at her. "My *what*?"

"Testosterone level. You're extremely virile. That's part of what makes your sculptures so exciting. Virile men are usually territorial like wolves."

"Wolves? Hey, I don't—"

"Last night we talked about my other lovers, but it was fairly abstract. This morning you had to wear the garment, or the skin, in a way, of someone who had encroached on what you temporarily claim as yours. Naturally, you got a little snarly."

"Oh, my God." He grinned at her. "You're too much."

"I happen to think I'm on target!"

"I happen to think you're adorable." He gathered her close. "We used to have ten minutes for this but after that testosterone speech we only have about eight. I might have to do it with most of your clothes on."

Although he was exciting the hell out of her, she pretended that she didn't need what he was offering. "Grady, this isn't necessary. We should just get ready and go."

"It is necessary." He edged her over to the sofa. "We can accomplish this right here."

"You're making it sound like a chore to be completed."

"Believe me, it's no chore." He guided her down to the sofa and urged her back on the cushions. "I've decided I like the wolf analogy you came up with, after all. Since I was subjected to wearing the skin of my rival, I need to reassert my dominance." He pushed up her skirt and pulled down her panties.

"This position is awkward." But her heart was beating like a snare drum.

"No, it's not." He worked one of the leg openings of her panties over her foot. "That does it." He stroked her and slid a finger into her. "I think you might be more interested in this makeup sex than you're letting on."

"My mother wanted to know if you called because we were going to have a quickie."

A condom appeared, no doubt tucked in the pocket of his borrowed robe. "Smart woman, your mother." He rolled it on and moved between her trembling thighs. "The alpha wolf is taking control. Just go with it." And he drove into her with all the authority of the leader of the pack.

She responded with a moan of ecstasy. She'd known from the moment she'd walked in to find him wearing the black robe that barely covered his magnificent physique that this would be the final outcome. Whether he called it makeup sex or alpha sex didn't matter.

Nothing mattered but the firm thrust of his cock and the orgasm he would soon coax from her quivering body. Bracing herself against the cushions, she rose to meet him. In this, the primitive language of male and female, they understood each other. Their communication was exquisitely timed to the rhythm of his strokes and the undulation of her hips.

His voice was thick with passion. "I love how this feels."

"I love how you feel." She gasped. "Moving inside me. Ah, like that. Like *that*." She tipped over the edge, falling into a whirlpool of color and light.

He followed soon after with a deep groan of satisfaction. As he shuddered in her arms, his happiness became hers and in that brief moment life was perfect.

THEY TOOK SHOWERS in different bathrooms or they would never have made it to her parents' house. Arriving at her childhood home after having explosive sex with the man who walked in with her was a surreal experience made even more so when her mother clearly was in the know.

She gave Sapphire a big hug. "You're looking so happy."

"I'm a happy person."

"But tonight you're especially so." She turned to Grady with a wide smile. "How generous of you to be a part of the Art Barn's fund-raiser." She held out her hand. "You're a credit to your alma mater, even though I never had you in class. Why was that?"

He took her hand in both of his. "Because I was young and stupid, Mrs. Ferguson."

"Please call me Jane. You're not a kid anymore and I can tell you're older and wiser."

"I sure hope so, ma'am."

Sapphire had expected her mother to be friendly. After all, she wanted Grady to talk to her classes sometime this fall. But the level of welcome was even greater than she'd counted on.

Her mom had put on her favorite dress, a purple caftan embroidered in gold that complemented her salt-and-pepper hair. She wore it with lots of gold jewelry and she was tall, almost as tall as Sapphire's father, so the outfit made her look like a queen.

Her bangles jingled and sparkled as she gestured toward Sapphire's dad, a lanky, balding man who liked wearing black turtlenecks and faded jeans. "You remember Stan, don't you? His band played for several of the school dances."

"I sure do remember." Grady shook his hand. "Good to see you again, sir. Sapphire tells me you still have a jazz band."

"Yep, and we're busier than ever. It's great to see you again, too. Impressive what you've accomplished, son, and I want to personally thank you for driving up for the silent auction. People really appreciate it and I know Sapphire was turning cartwheels when you agreed."

"Happy to do it."

Her dad had always been a jolly sort, so his effusive greeting wasn't a surprise. He entertained for a living and everyone he met was a new friend. Maybe her mom's reaction wasn't so shocking, either. She admired talented people, especially when they were focused. She'd probably heard from a couple of the co-op members by now and no doubt they'd raved about him.

Conversation flowed easily during dinner and by the end of the meal she had no doubt that both her parents liked Grady very much. He'd readily agreed to talk to her mother's classes in the fall and possibly again in the spring.

They were at the door saying their goodbyes when the discussion turned to her mother's entry in the silent auction. Grady wanted to see the weaving she planned to donate, so she took him back to her studio for a quick look.

After they left, her dad chuckled. "Your guy was a hit, Sapphie." He was the only person in the world who called her that, but a nickname from her dad was an expression of love and affection, so she treasured it.

"He's not really mine, Dad."

"Maybe not yet, but I can tell he wants to be. I recognize that look. He thinks you hung the moon. Which of course you did, so that makes him smarter than the other schmucks you brought home."

"You didn't like any of them, either? I know Mom didn't, but you like everybody."

"I like everybody until they prove they're dumb as a box of rocks. Anybody who doesn't appreciate your value falls into that category. I've only spent one evening with Grady and there's a lot I don't know about the guy. But I've already learned the most important thing about him. He thinks you're fantastic." He looked into her eyes. "It's important, Sapphie."

She'd never received romantic advice from her dad before. She had a feeling this might be the one and only time she would. "I'll remember that."

12

"THEY LIKE YOU." Sapphire started her truck and backed out of her parents' driveway.

"I like them, too. They're great." If Jane and Stan were in charge, they'd make sure he had a prominent place in their daughter's life. But they weren't in charge and he wouldn't wish them to be. If she didn't make her own decisions, she wouldn't be the same independent woman he admired.

"Are you still planning to work tonight?"

"Yep. If I don't, I'll be worried about rushing the sculpture and I'd like to take it to her tomorrow night." He glanced at her classic profile illuminated by the dashboard lights. She was so beautiful it made his heart hurt. "Want to come with me?"

She hesitated. "Do Rosie and Herb know anything about...us?"

"I doubt it. I haven't talked to them since I got here. I didn't want to take a chance that I'd slip and mention the sculpture."

"Or me?"

"I didn't consciously decide not to tell them about

you, but if Rosie thought I had a girlfriend, even a temporary one, she'd be here in a shot."

"How come?"

He laughed. "She has this old-fashioned idea that
each of her boys needs to find a good woman and live
happily-ever-after. She's more set on that than my own
mother. I guess it's because Rosie's had a great marriage and my mom had to make her way through a
couple of losers."

"Hmm."

"What?"

"So what will Rosie think if you show up with me
in tow?"

"She'll pick up on the fact that I think you're pretty
special. I'm sure your folks did."

"They did, which makes my point. Let's not complicate this any further. I don't think it's a good idea for
me to go out to Thunder Mountain with you."

Her answer disappointed him more than he wanted
to admit. "Don't you want to see Rosie's reaction to
the sculpture?"

"Yeah, but—"

"Then come with me. It'll be fine."

She sighed. "If I thought she couldn't read you like
a book, I might consider it, but I don't want to get her
hopes up. When you get back, you can tell me all about
it."

"All right." Maybe he shouldn't have said anything
about Rosie's dream of seeing all her foster boys settled. No, he was glad he'd said it. Taking her out there
without mentioning it would have been unfair.

But he'd wanted her to be on hand when Rosie caught
sight of the wolf sculpture, and yeah, that was selfish. He'd hoped Rosie's reaction would make Sapphire

like him a little more. He was no different from a ten-year-old doing tricks on the monkey bars to impress a pretty girl.

"I'm sorry, Grady. I just don't think it's a good idea."

"Probably not."

"I had to let my mom know about us since you're staying in my house instead of at Ben and Molly's, where she'd planned to contact you. But going to see Rosie would open up a whole new can of worms."

"I hate to say it but you're right. The last time I brought a girl out there, it was senior prom. Taking you to meet Rosie and Herb would be seen as a significant move." No point in kidding himself. He'd wanted to raise the stakes but Sapphire hadn't let him.

"My dad's band played for that prom."

"Yeah, they did. I wonder if we appreciated what a great band we had. Probably not."

"You might not have then, but you do when you look back on it." She smiled. "I'll bet my mom's hoping you'll tell her students that you regret not taking her class when you were at SHS."

"Don't worry. I will."

"Thanks for agreeing to do it. I know she's thrilled."

He was glad to do it for Jane, but he had ulterior motives. Keeping the connection with Jane meant keeping the connection with Sapphire. "I was flattered. I never thought of myself as a role model before."

"I'm sure that's one of the reasons they like you. You're modest."

He'd had enough of that kind of talk. He didn't want her thinking of him as some effing choirboy. "About my art, always. About my sexual attributes, on the other hand…" He reached over and stroked her thigh.

"Stop that before I run us into a ditch."

"Or you could drive into a ditch on purpose and we could climb into the bed of your truck."

"Don't tell me you brought a condom with you for the trip to my folks' house?"

He pulled it out of his pocket and tossed it on the dash. "But sadly, we're not going to use it to have sex in the back of your truck. Never fear, though, I'll have it handy when I finish up for the night." He scooped it up and shoved it back in his pocket.

"I believe you." Her laughter had a tremor of excitement in it.

Well, good. At least he still had that going for him. "Are you going to work tonight, too?"

"I thought about it, but I'm pretty well caught up. Instead I'll stay home and clean."

He winced. "Cat hair."

"It's been on my mind. Might as well take care of it."

"That's just wrong. My cat, my cat hair. I'll do it."

"I appreciate the offer but you said you needed to work on Rosie's sculpture so you won't feel as if you rushed it."

"True. Maybe when I get back."

"Seriously?" She glanced at him. "With a hot condom in your pocket?"

"Maybe not. How about tomorrow?"

"We'll be up early to feed the cats, both the ferals and Gandalf. Tomorrow night you'll be going out to Rosie's. Think of it this way. If I clean the bathroom and wash all the towels, we can shower together in the morning."

"That's a powerful argument, lady. But I still hate to stick you with the job. I'll find a way to make it up to you when I get back tonight."

"I'm sure you will." She pulled into her driveway,

turned off the engine and took something out of her purse. "Here's a spare key."

"Was this—"

"Don't read anything into it."

"Okay." But he already had. He'd bet money this key had belonged to the cheater. He wouldn't care except her old boyfriends had left a toxic legacy. Anything associated with them was a reminder of the mess he faced because of their bad behavior.

He hopped out of the truck in time to go around and hoist her down. Drawing her close, he gazed into her starlit face. "I'm not going to kiss you, because if I do, I won't leave."

"And I want you to leave, cowboy." She gave him a playful little push. "Get the hell out of here. We both have work to do."

Backing away, he touched the brim of his hat. "See you soon."

THAT HAD BEEN his sincere intention. But it was after three in the morning when he picked up his phone to check the time. His string of obscenities woke Gandalf, who'd been sleeping peacefully on his cat tree.

"Sorry, cat." He walked over and ran his hand over the soft fur. "I just blew it." The sculpture was nearly finished. A couple more hours should do the trick, but he'd promised Sapphire he'd be back to make sweet love to her as a thank-you for cleaning up the cat hair. She'd probably fallen asleep cursing his worthless ass.

He considered staying to complete the sculpture since he wouldn't make any points showing up now. But that didn't feel right. He'd go back, use the cheater's key and climb into bed as quietly as possible so he wouldn't wake her. It was the least he could do.

Driving through the silent streets, he was torn between guilt and elation. Rosie's sculpture looked good. Parts of it had been a challenge but he'd met those challenges tonight and he was proud of the result. In the process, he'd forgotten all about Sapphire.

How could he do that? He'd counted on his hormones to keep him aware that he had a sexy woman waiting for him. He'd never wanted any woman as much as he wanted her, so if thoughts of her hadn't penetrated his single-minded absorption in his work, nothing would.

What if she was right, and he had a fatal flaw like all the other guys? He might not be disorganized and immature. He certainly didn't have a superiority complex and he couldn't imagine cheating on her. But he'd allowed his work to blot out all thoughts of his promise to return to her tonight.

Worse yet, he'd probably do it again, either with her or the next girlfriend. His concentration on his art had been an issue more than once with the women he'd dated. He'd considered himself so much better than the jerks she'd been with, but had any of them been capable of forgetting her completely?

He couldn't even claim she'd been on the fringes of his mind. He hadn't thought of her once as he'd labored over the sculpture into the wee hours. She likely wouldn't be comforted to know he hadn't thought of Rosie, either.

Using his devotion to his foster mother was tempting, but it wasn't the reason he'd kept working. His foster mother had inspired the original concept, but after he'd fully involved himself in the process, the piece had become an end in itself. He loved his work and he wondered for the first time if that precluded him loving anything or anyone else.

The house was dark. By the time he'd put away his tools and started the drive back here, the clock on his dash had shown him that four o'clock wasn't far away. Her alarm was set for six. He'd mucked up whatever chance he'd had to convince her he was the right guy for her.

Because he wasn't. A woman like Sapphire deserved better than being stood up when she'd spent the evening cleaning cat hair out of her bathroom. He thought of the pile of towels he'd left and the fur in the bathtub drain. He'd never mentioned Gandalf's love of showers.

He parked behind her purple truck and remembered the moment when he'd held her close and made that asinine comment about not kissing her because he'd never leave if he did. She'd sent him on his way and encouraged him to get his work done. She'd trusted him to keep his part of the bargain.

The cheater's key slid smoothly into the lock and he let himself into the quiet house and locked the door behind him. The place smelled of soap and lemon oil. As his eyes adjusted to the darkness, he saw the black robe lying over the arm of the sofa. He picked it up and sniffed. She'd washed that, too, and left it for him.

He felt lower than a snake's belly. Deciding to undress in the living room because that would make less noise, he carefully took off his clothes, folded them and laid them on the sofa. Then he put on the robe she'd readied for him. His incurable optimism prompted him to transfer the condom from his jeans to the robe.

Maybe he should bed down on the sofa and not disturb her. But that seemed wrong, as if he wanted to distance himself from her. If he had any decency, he would distance himself and let her find a nice guy who didn't have a creative bone in his body.

But whatever happened between them, he'd never want her to think that he didn't want her. He might not deserve her. In fact, he was pretty damn certain on that point. But that didn't mean he didn't crave her with every fiber of his being, selfish bastard that he was.

Luckily, he knew the bedroom layout by now and even in the dark he could find the bed. She'd always favored the right side, so he felt confident in taking off the robe and sliding in on the left. But she must have switched positions, because he bumped up against her warm body and she immediately came awake.

"Grady?"

"Shh. Go back to sleep. I'll climb in on the other side."

"No." She grabbed for him and caught hold of his arm. "I took this side so I'd know when you got in. Let me scoot over. Are you okay?"

His breath stalled. He'd pictured her angry, not worried. He slipped under the covers and gathered her close. "I'm fine. I got involved in the sculpture and lost track of time. I'm so, so sorry."

"I told myself that was what happened." She snuggled against him. "I've seen how you focus. But I have a good imagination, so I dreamed up all sorts of tragic scenarios. I'm glad none of those were true."

He was stunned. "You're not upset with me?"

"How could I be? You were lost in your work. It happens." She wrapped her arms around him and promptly fell asleep.

Holding her close, he stared into the darkness. He'd found a woman who understood his preoccupation with his work, which was a certified miracle. He'd been prepared to exit her life because that was the decent thing to do when he couldn't be the man she needed.

But she'd just accepted the single worst thing about him without so much as a whimper or a whine. He couldn't have predicted that in a million years. He'd known she was special, but he hadn't known how special. She wasn't going to get rid of him easily.

HE SLEPT THROUGH her alarm. She must have showered and dressed upstairs, because the first noise he heard was the sound of her truck starting up. *Shitfire.* Leaping out of bed, he was about to race after her when it occurred to him he was naked. The neighbors hadn't caught him having sex with her on the front porch, but they'd likely notice if he ran down her driveway with his junk jiggling.

Rushing into the freshly cleaned bathroom, he found the note she'd taped to the mirror. *Morning, Sleeping Beauty. Take your time. I'll feed Gandalf. We'll see you when you get there.*

Nothing else. No smiley face, no *Love, Sapphire.* No signature at all. But then, it wasn't like he wouldn't know who'd written it. She wouldn't want to put anything in writing that could be misinterpreted as mushy.

She didn't sound mad, though. Considering he'd stumbled in at four in the morning and had slept straight through the alarm and her preparations to leave, she had a right to be mildly irritated, at least.

Instead she was acting like a person who understood what happened when the work took hold and wouldn't let go, as if she'd been in that same place. That was exciting to think about. Ever since the day three weeks ago when he'd come over to the Art Barn with Cade, he'd known he and Sapphire had a sexual connection. What a bonus if she got him.

With no Gandalf to join him in the shower, he made

it out of the house in no time. On the way to the Art Barn he detoured past the bakery and bought a couple dozen assorted doughnuts. Then he picked up a fast-food egg sandwich and coffee from the drive-through and ate on the way.

He was feeling reasonably human by the time he parked in front of the barn. Only three other vehicles were there, so the whole group hadn't arrived yet. Sapphire, George and Arlene were in residence. He'd identified Arlene and George as Sapphire's core supporters of the program.

He grabbed the box of doughnuts and walked through the front door. Then he paused and listened to the sound of artists at work—Arlene singing under her breath as she painted, George sanding a piece of wood in preparation for carving, Sapphire's wheel humming. He enjoyed the energy of this place. Working alone had its value, but this had been a nice change.

George stuck his head out. "Hey, Grady. Whatcha got?"

"Something for the coffee break. Pretend you never saw it."

"Gotcha." He went back to work.

Grady set the treats on the desk in the office and was in the process of getting a cup of coffee to take back to his stall when Gandalf rubbed up against his leg. "Hey, buddy!" He put down his mug and picked up the cat. He got a kick out of knowing Gandalf had heard or smelled him and had come to say hello.

The cat purred like there was no tomorrow as Grady scratched under his chin. "Looks like you survived staying alone for a little while. Wasn't long, though. Tonight you'll have to hang out by yourself for a good twelve hours. But at least you have a whole barn to explore. Gotta be more interesting than staying in a bathroom."

Gandalf closed his eyes and stretched his neck in ecstasy. Whatever trauma he'd suffered while he was on his own seemed forgotten. The shelter vet had mentioned that he'd need a cat carrier for the long drive to Cody, but Grady hated the idea of sticking him in an enclosed space. He'd look for one with mesh sides so Gandalf could see him.

"Hey, I need to get to work, buddy." After one last scratch, he put the cat down and picked up his mug of coffee. Gandalf trotted at his heels on the way to his space.

Arlene leaned around her easel and waved. He smiled and gave her a thumbs-up. Sapphire was intent on her wheel as red clay responded to her touch, rising to form a vase that resembled the hourglass shape of a woman. He paused for a bare second, not wanting to interrupt. Besides, the sight of her molding that clay got him hot.

He hadn't felt her hands on his naked body since yesterday morning, and that was his own damned fault. Moving on, he glanced over at George's workbench and exchanged a quick salute with the wood-carver. The heron Grady coveted had a big red *sold* sign hanging around its neck.

Gandalf leaped to the top of his cat tree and curled up as if he'd lived in the barn for years instead of hours. Grady chuckled at the cat's smug expression as he stared down from his perch. Finally, though, he couldn't put off the moment any longer. It was time to take a look at the wolves in the light of day. Something that he thought was genius at three in the morning might have turned to crap by the time he'd had some sleep.

Setting his hat brim-side-up on a nearby shelf, he

took a deep breath and turned toward the sculpture. His heart beat faster. It was good, really good. Thank God for that, because if it hadn't been, he wouldn't have had time to fix it. He had a little more to do, but not much. He could finish this morning and then start organizing what he'd need for the cougar.

He grabbed his welding gloves and his goggles, intent on those few touches—an ear that wasn't quite what he wanted and a tail that needed adjustment. Minor tweaks.

"Before you start…"

He glanced up.

Sapphire stood just outside his area wiping clay from her hands with a damp cloth. "Uh-oh. You've already started. I can see that from the look in your eyes. It's okay. We can talk later." She turned to leave.

"No, wait. Don't go away." He set down the goggles and gloves. "You deserve an apology…" He paused to lower his voice. They weren't exactly alone. "I was supposed to help you with the cats this morning." *And make love to you last night and again this morning in the shower.*

"No worries." She smiled. "Fred came over and sniffed me."

"You're kidding!" And he'd missed it.

"He's definitely changing his ways. Last night I blinked at him and he blinked back, and this morning—"

"Hold on. What's blinking have to do with it?"

"I learned that from a shelter volunteer. If a cat blinks at you, it's a sign they're willing to be friends. The human can start it off and see if the cat responds. It's a good way to find out how socialized they are."

"I'll be damned. Never heard that before."

"Anyway, it's possible that you were right. Fred

might have noticed your interaction with Gandalf and maybe it triggered a distant memory of human interaction. But that's not what I came over to talk about."

"I'm glad to hear about Fred, though. I know you like him." He needed to hold her more than he needed to breathe. This definitely wasn't the time. He had hours to wait for that privilege.

"The important part is coaxing him to like me. I think he's getting there."

"Good." He was miles ahead of that tuxedo cat. He'd shot way past the liking stage and was fairly sure he'd entered love territory.

"I came over to ask if I can go out to Thunder Mountain with you."

He couldn't have been more surprised if she'd pulled out castanets and launched into a flamenco dance routine. "Well, sure, but...I thought you had reservations."

"I did. I do. But then I came in this morning and saw your wolves." She held his gaze. "They're magnificent."

"Thank you." Her sincere praise affected him enough that he had to clear his throat. "Glad you like them."

"I love them and she will, too. The moment she first sees them will be very special. I can't bear to miss it."

"Great." He sucked in a breath. "That's great." Now *he* felt like pulling out castanets and launching into a flamenco dance routine. Or better yet, he wanted to pick her up and whirl her around like guys did in the movies. But too much enthusiasm might freak her out and telegraph their situation to the others. He settled for a smile. "I'll text Rosie and tell her to set an extra place for dinner."

"You're not going to say who it's for?"

"You tell me. Which way would you rather play it?"

"Tell her I'll be with you. I don't want a little surprise

of me showing up to take anything away from the big surprise of the wolves."

"Okay." This was shaping up to be a fantastic night. "Can I bring anything?"

"I would say a bottle of Baileys because she loves that with coffee, but apparently, she's still working on a case of it three of the guys got her last summer. You don't have to bring anything."

"But I've never been out there. I don't like arriving empty-handed."

"Then how about a bottle of wine? That always works."

"What kind?"

"Anything. Just some decent brand. They're not picky."

She brightened. "I know!" Then she looked uncertain. "But maybe that's not such a good idea."

"What?"

"I have this bottle of two-hundred-dollar wine I've never opened…"

"Hell, yes. Bring it."

"That wouldn't bother you?"

"Not a bit. Terrific idea." And maybe before he left, he'd talk her into giving away the shirt and burning the Valentine's Day card. Progress was being made.

13

SAPPHIRE FOUND OUT that Grady's truck had a CD player, so she brought one of Amethyst's albums for the trip out to the ranch. Her sister tended to sing upbeat tunes and Sapphire figured they'd need a distraction since they'd both be nervous and excited.

The wolf sculpture lay in the back wrapped in a tarp, secured with rope and cushioned by a thick piece of carpet. Fortunately, the bundle sat low in the truck bed, virtually out of sight unless someone leaned over the side to peer in. They'd arrive after sunset, so the gathering darkness should keep Rosie and Herb from noticing anything.

"Your sister has an awesome voice," Grady said after Amethyst's first number. "Thanks for bringing the CD. I feel like a Mexican jumping bean but the music helps."

"I listen to her albums whenever I need to get out of my own head."

"She just goes by Amethyst?"

"Yeah. It's a great name. Stands on its own. She's a local talent now but I predict she'll get her big break."

"With a voice like that, she should."

They talked about her sister's career during the next

song, but then they lapsed into silence. Amethyst's music usually had that effect on people. They wanted to shut up and listen to the lyrics, most of which her sister wrote. Some of the tunes were love songs and a couple of times Sapphire caught Grady glancing over at her.

She wasn't an idiot. She knew he was falling for her, and if she allowed herself to, she'd fall for him. He'd be easy to love, this broad-shouldered cowboy with the drive and talent to make beautiful art and an earthy sensuality that turned sex into an adventure. He was exactly her type, and that was the problem.

If he lived in town, she could get to know him better and watch for that relationship-wrecker trait to show up. Or not. But he didn't live here and a week wasn't enough time to uncover all facets of his personality.

She'd learned he could get lost in his work, which could be seen as a negative, although she didn't consider it one. He was mildly possessive, but she couldn't blame him for objecting to the shirt. He was okay with her bringing Edgar's wine. She'd debated whether to retrieve the bottle afterward, but maybe she didn't need these reminders so much anymore. Taking it back with them would be kind of dorky.

The sun had dropped below the Bighorn Mountains by the time they drove up to the one-story ranch house. Grady turned off the engine. "This is it, the place that I called home for two years."

"I can see why you loved it." Sapphire took in the long front porch lined with Adirondack chairs painted in the academy colors of brown and green. The porch was empty but she pictured it filled with kids drinking soda and soaking up the ambiance.

"You can't see the meadow or the cabins from here." He rolled down the window. "But you can hear the kids." Music and laughter drifted on the evening breeze. "Man, that brings back memories." He inhaled deeply. "They must be burning logs in the fire pit. Probably toasting marshmallows."

She smiled. "Sure you wouldn't rather go down there and eat burned marshmallows with the kids?"

"Nope. I can also smell Rosie's meat loaf. It's good to be home." He paused. "That might sound strange when I only lived here two years, but we moved a lot when I was a kid. Mom would get a raise and we'd pack up and go to a nicer rental. I never lived in the house she and my stepdad own, so this is the one constant from my early years."

"And a comforting one, I'll bet."

"Yep." He gazed at the barn a short distance away. A couple of slender kids walked out and closed the double doors, then slid a beam across to secure them. "They've finished their evening chores. I miss having horses around. I used to ride every chance I got."

"Could you have them on your property?"

"I could, but I'll monitor how things go with the cat first. As you discovered, I can disappear into my work and animals need a routine."

"I think you could figure that out."

"Probably." He glanced at her. "By the way, Cade will be eating with us. Lexi's conducting a riding clinic down in Casper."

"Catch me up on that situation. Are they engaged or not?"

"Not yet. Cade wants to get married but she's reluctant until he proves that he's domesticated and won't expect her to handle what used to be considered women's work. That's why he was buying art three weeks ago."

"Fascinating." Sapphire grinned. "Too bad Lexi won't be here. Back in high school she treated him like a god."

"Yeah. She's over that." He reached for his door handle.

"Wait. Before we go in, what's the plan?"

"Oh, right. I got caught up in nostalgia and forgot to tell you. Cade and I worked it out on the phone this afternoon. His cabin's a short walk from here. After we say hi to everyone, he'll suggest going up there to show me how it looks. Instead we'll unload the sculpture."

"What about me?"

"You can go with us or stay and talk to Rosie and Herb."

"I'm going with you, cowboy. If I stay with Rosie, she's liable to ask some pointed questions."

"She might, but she means well."

"Of course she does. She loves you and wants the best for you. I just don't want to be asked about my intentions."

"Then you can say you're dying to see how the artwork looks in Cade's cabin."

"I actually am now that I know he bought it to prove he's domesticated."

"He'd probably take us up there for real after dinner if you want. I just thought you might want to head back to your house."

In the soft twilight she turned to gaze at him. She couldn't see his face very well but she could feel his heat. "Now that you mention it, I'm not that curious to see the inside of Cade's cabin."

He smiled. "Me, either."

They were halfway to the porch steps when Rosie came out the door followed by Herb. Short, plump and blond, she looked fairly harmless, but Sapphire had heard things over the years. You didn't want to get on Rosie's bad side and the quickest way to do that was by hurting someone Rosie loved.

"I thought I heard your truck, Grady Magee!" Rosie hurried down the steps. "But then you didn't come in, so I had to find out what was keeping you!"

"We got to talking."

"That's nice." Rosie smiled as if she liked hearing that. "Now come here and give me a hug, you rascal!"

As he leaned down and gathered her into his arms, Sapphire knew she was already in trouble. Rosie likely had put her own spin on Grady's "We got to talking" comment and had concluded they cared about each other. She wasn't wrong. Watching Grady hug his foster mom warmed Sapphire's heart and tightened her throat. She'd failed to maintain an emotional distance from this man.

Grady moved on to embrace Herb, a wiry guy with thinning hair, and Rosie turned her attention to Sapphire. "I'm so glad you could join us tonight!" She took Sapphire's hands in hers. "Thanks for coaxing our boy to come up for your fund-raiser."

"Yeah, thanks." Cade came down the steps grinning all the way. "It's always a treat to see your ugly mug, Magee." He exchanged a bro hug with Grady.

"And I'm so happy about this event, Sapphire." Herb came over and shook her hand. "I really admire what you're doing. I became a large-animal vet because the overpopulation of dogs and cats broke my heart. Had to work in a different area."

"Needless to say, Herb and I will be there Saturday night," Rosie said. "We're putting Cade in charge of the kids."

Cade laughed. "Yeah, we're going to do drugs and

rent porn. It'll be epic." He clapped Grady on the shoulder. "Hey, I was just thinking you haven't seen how the artwork looks in the cabin."

"Sure haven't, but I'd love to."

Sapphire picked up her cue. "I wouldn't mind checking that out since I was the one who sold it to you."

"We could make a quick trip up there right now." Cade turned to Rosie and Herb. "Unless dinner's ready."

"The meat loaf needs another fifteen minutes," Rosie said. "If you want to take Grady and Sapphire up to see your cabin, go ahead."

"Then I will. Come on, guys. We'll take a secret route to avoid running into any teenagers along the way."

Sapphire lifted the wine bottle she held. "Before we leave, let me give you this, Rosie. But if you've already opened something to serve with dinner, no problem."

Rosie looked at the bottle. "I haven't opened anything yet and red goes great with meat loaf. I've never tasted this one, so thanks! We'll try something new tonight." She and Herb walked back into the house.

Cade watched them go inside. "Give them a few minutes. Let them get involved in setting the table and opening the wine." He glanced over at Sapphire. "I could be mistaken, but that looked like a bottle I decided was out of my league."

"It was a gift. I could never find the right time to open it but tonight seemed like the perfect situation."

"That's very cool. And even cooler that you didn't tell them it was expensive stuff. Now, let's get the masterpiece out of the Torch Man's pickup."

Sapphire laughed but Grady rolled his eyes.

Cade moved closer to Sapphire and lowered his voice, but not by much. "I think he secretly likes us to call him that but he pretends not to. It got started at the wedding and you know how these things go."

"Which is forever." Grady lowered the tailgate, climbed in and began untying the ropes. "When it comes to running something into the ground, nobody does it better than the Thunder Mountain guys."

"Not *guys*." Cade looked pained. "Thunder Mountain *Brotherhood*."

"I remember that from high school." Sapphire had thought it was touching that the foster boys had come up with a way to reclaim a sense of family. "It was you, Damon and… Who was the third one?"

"Finn. He's a brewer up in Seattle now. It used to be just the three of us, but we've expanded the name to include everybody. Torch Man here keeps forgetting."

"Torch Man is ready to take this thing out of the truck whenever you finish working your jaw, Gallagher."

"Excuse me, sweet lady. Time to use my impressive muscles." Cade rounded the back of the truck. "Where're we going with it?"

"I thought you had a spot picked out."

"I sort of do." He vaulted into the truck. "Tell me the dimensions again."

"Five feet, seven and three-quarters inches long, three feet, two and a quarter inches high."

"Okay." Cade hopped down and began pacing along the front of the house.

Sapphire didn't think it belonged in front of the house at all, but this wasn't her decision.

"Here." Cade gestured toward a spot beside the porch steps.

Grady shook his head. "We can't put it there."

"Why not? It'll show up real good."

"Rosie likes her little flower bed."

"Then maybe at the far end of the house. Or how about on the porch?"

Grady blew out a breath. "Definitely not on the porch."

"The far end?"

Sapphire finally couldn't keep her suggestion to herself any longer, and besides, they were running out of time. "Under that pine tree in the side yard," she said. "It would be perfect there."

Both men looked at her. Then they turned in unison toward the side yard.

"She's right," Cade said.

"Yeah, she is." Grady resettled his Stetson. "It'll be more natural instead of sticking it somewhere out front. Thanks, Sapphire. Listen, while we get it off the truck, would you walk over and scope out the most level spot?"

She gazed up at him. "Wouldn't you rather back the truck over there so you don't have to carry it so far?"

Grady glanced at Cade and they both started laughing.

"Yeah," Grady said, wiping his eyes. "That would be the intelligent way to do it. Cade, why don't you and Sapphire find the spot while I back the truck over?"

"Of course, there's the chance Rosie will hear the truck," Sapphire said.

"She might." Cade scratched the back of his neck. "Hell, we need to get this done without giving ourselves a hernia. Let's risk it."

In moments she and Cade had found the spot and Grady backed right up to it. Then he and Cade used the carpet to pull the wrapped sculpture partway out. With much grunting and groaning, they lowered it to the ground.

"Heavy sonofabitch," Cade muttered.

"That's the idea." Grady was breathing hard, which could be a combination of effort and excitement. "That way it'll stay put. Let's—"

"What in God's name is going on out here?" Rosie walked around the truck with Herb right behind her. "Are you fixing to bury a dead body under my pine tree, Grady Magee?"

"If he is, then rigor mortis has already set in," Herb said.

Rosie eyed Cade. "I thought you were taking them up to your cabin."

Cade went over and put an arm around her. "That was what you call a subterfuge. We're trying to do something special here, so how about you and Dad go back inside and we'll call you when we're ready?"

She turned to Herb. "Are you in on this?"

"I know nothing about it, Rosie. I'm as clueless as you are."

She continued to stand in the circle of Cade's arm while she stared hard at Grady, who had laid his hand on the wrapped sculpture. Suddenly she covered her eyes and began to cry. "It's my sculpture! That's what it is! Oh, my God."

Cade sent a pleading glance Herb's way and he took his sobbing wife in his arms.

"I won't look," she wailed as she buried her wet face against Herb's shoulder.

"I won't, either." Herb bowed his head. "Finish up with what you have to do and tell us when."

Sapphire hurried over to pull the tarp away while Grady and Cade lifted the sculpture. She bundled it in her arms and went closer to watch as the two men wrestled with the base until Grady was satisfied with the angle.

"That's good," he murmured.

Cade stepped a couple of feet away. "Wow," he said quietly. Glancing over his shoulder at Sapphire, he mouthed the word again.

She nodded. Her heart pounded as she wondered what Rosie would say. She'd bet Grady's heart was beating as fast as hers.

His hand trembled as he picked off some fibers left by the tarp. Moving away so he wouldn't block Rosie and Herb's view, he took a deep breath. "You can look."

Herb raised his head and Rosie turned in his arms. They both gasped and Rosie began to cry again. But this time she rushed into Grady's arms. "It's b-beautiful!" She hugged him tight and he hugged her back. "A mama wolf with her pups! How did you know that's what I'd want?"

His voice was thick. "Good guess."

"Oh, Grady." She gazed up at him, tears streaking her face. "I'm sorry if I spoiled your wonderful surprise."

He smiled. "You didn't."

Sapphire had to work hard to keep from crying herself. Grady had nailed it. Instinctively, she knew that of all the sculptures he'd created, some immense and worth untold amounts of money, this relatively modest one he'd made for Rosie was the most important piece he'd ever done.

She wanted to hug him, too, but that wasn't appropriate. She could congratulate him later, when they were alone. For now, she could watch with a full heart as Herb joined Grady and Rosie's embrace. Rosie had to examine every inch of the sculpture while she raved about the cleverness of each part and the beauty of the whole. Herb contributed his share of praise and kept patting Grady on the back.

Finally, Cade walked up and pulled Grady into a bear hug. "Incredible job, Torch Man. You impress me, big guy."

"We'll need a spotlight," Rosie said. "A low one." She turned to Sapphire. "Would you consider helping us set that up? You must have lots of experience with lighting artwork."

"I'd love to. We might have to wait until after Saturday, though."

"That's fine! I just want to be able to see it at night, but I can wait until next week. The beam needs to be positioned so it shows the wolves to the best advantage. I love that little one with his paw over his nose! That's so adorable. How do you think of such things, Grady?"

"I didn't." Grady smiled at Sapphire. "It was Sapphire's idea."

Rosie looked over at her. "You got to watch him make this, didn't you?"

"I sure did. It was inspiring."

"I can imagine." Her attention went back to the sculpture. "I could look at it forever. I hate to go in."

"But the meat loaf's not getting any younger," Herb said.

Rosie sighed. "That's true. If we don't take it out of the oven pretty soon, it'll be all dried up. Let's go eat. Later we can come back out with a flashlight and look at my wolves some more."

Everyone followed Rosie back to the kitchen. Sapphire discovered that was where they ate unless they had a crowd. They all helped get the food on the table and Grady opened Sapphire's wine. To her surprise, he held out the cork.

"Want this?" His brown eyes relayed a challenge.

She shook her head. "You can toss it."

"Maybe we should save it," Rosie said. "After all, this is a red-letter day."

"Then take it with my blessing." Sapphire's gaze met Grady's. She knew that look by now. He wanted to kiss her. And that was just for starters. This kitchen was cozy and welcoming, but she could hardly wait to leave it.

14

"THAT WAS A real high, giving the sculpture to Rosie and having you there with me." Grady had pleaded exhaustion in order to get out the door with Sapphire rather than stay for a game of poker and more viewings of Rosie's wolves. Technically, he should have been worn-out, considering how little sleep he'd had recently. Instead he was strung tight as a hunter's bow.

They were finally on the road and he fought the urge to pull onto a side road and make love to Sapphire. But the cab didn't have enough room to do it right and the bed of his truck was a mess. She'd worn a skirt with bright red hibiscus flowers on it and a red blouse, neither of which should be scrunched up in the cab or subjected to the grime in the back.

"I'm so glad I asked to be there."

Her musical voice stroked his already sensitized nerves. He wanted to hear that voice urging him on as he thrust into her. He passed narrow dirt roads that he'd used as teenage make-out spots. Back then he'd outfitted the bed of his truck with a self-inflating air mattress that he could deploy at a moment's notice.

"Rosie loved those wolves, Grady."

"I do believe she did." Part of his desire for sex was a response to everyone's admiration of his work. He needed to let off steam and dispel the nervous energy that successfully completing and delivering a project created in him. He liked having sex at moments like this, but sometimes that hadn't been an option, so he'd made substitutions—downing a couple of six packs, maybe taking a nude swim in an icy lake or going on a midnight run through the pines.

Tonight he had the option with a terrific woman who might actually understand the untamed emotions pumping through him. He also had a condom since he'd made it a practice to carry one at all times this week. All he lacked was a viable horizontal surface. Hell, he'd settle for a vertical surface but his truck needed a wash, so he wasn't going to take her up against the fender.

He was approaching the last secluded dirt road he knew about when he remembered the blanket he'd rolled up and tucked behind his seat. He'd found it on sale at least a year ago. It was more a plush throw than a blanket and for some reason the leopard spots had appealed to him.

After buying it, he'd tucked it behind his seat and forgotten about it. Why would he remember? He'd had no girlfriend in the past year and no emergencies where he'd been stranded in icy winter conditions. But he had an emergency now. He turned off on the dirt road.

"Grady?"

"There's something I have to do."

"If you need to answer nature's call, go right ahead. I won't look."

"I want to answer a different call from nature, more a call of the wild." He searched for a break in the trees. There. A clearing he remembered from the old days.

With luck, it would still have some grassy spots. He pulled off the road.

"Is this about sex?"

"Yes, ma'am. I just remembered I have a blanket behind my seat. It's not very big but it'll protect you from the cold ground." He switched off the engine and glanced at her in the darkness. "Unless you don't want to."

"I want to." Lust added a dark, rich flavor to her words.

He let out a breath. "Thank God. Let me scout around and find a place for the blanket." He laid his hat on the dash and shut off the dome light. He'd learned early in his make-out career that nothing ruined the mood faster than the harsh brilliance of a dome light coming on when he opened the door. He'd never expected to use that information again, but here he was. "I'll come back for you."

"All right." Her voice was breathy.

Unsnapping his seat belt, he leaned over and cupped the back of her head. "I'm going crazy from wanting you. I'm a danger on the road." He captured her mouth and kissed her hard. Then he released her, climbed out and grabbed the blanket.

After letting his eyes adjust to the darkness, he scanned the clearing. His teenage instincts came back to him and he made his way to one of the few grassy areas. Spreading the throw over the ground reawakened that seventeen-year-old he used to be and his arousal strained against his fly.

He ignored the pain as he returned to the truck, opened the door and discovered that Sapphire had been busy in his absence. She wore nothing but a smile.

She held out her arms. "I thought I'd help things along."

"Oh, lady, what you do to me." He scooped her up and nudged the door closed with his shoulder.

"I have a fair idea."

"I'm about to give you all the information you need on that topic." He managed to lay her on the blanket without dropping her. Then he took off his shirt, rolled it up and bent down to tuck it under her head.

She caught his face in both hands. "Kiss me."

With a groan, he fell to his knees. The first contact with her warm lips snapped his control and he couldn't seem to stop kissing her. His hungry mouth sought the hollow of her throat, the curve of her shoulder, the fullness of her breasts.

He nipped and suckled his way down, then dipped his tongue in her navel, which made her squeal. He liked the sound so much that he did it again.

"I'm sensitive there!"

"Good." Sliding his hand between her thighs, he began an assault on her belly button with his tongue while his fingers kneaded the moist recesses that would soon welcome his cock. The more he explored, the wetter she became. She lifted her hips with a husky moan, inviting him deeper.

Women had wanted him before, but not like this. Sapphire's response was instantaneous, a rush of heat and desire that humbled him with her generosity. He recognized that she couldn't help wanting him just as he couldn't help wanting her, but he still considered her response a precious gift.

Learning what would make her come was such a joy. His tongue licking the tender crevice of her navel made her gasp and giggle, but it was the steady stroke of his fingers that teased an orgasm from her shuddering body. She called his name as she arched upward.

"I'm here." Sliding his fingers free, he eased between her thighs and covered her pulsing center with his mouth.

She said his name again, this time on a sigh of plea-sure. Savoring her juices, he settled in and took her up again until she was gasping and thrashing against the blanket. When she came a second time, he nuzzled and licked until her tremors subsided.

Now. Pushing to his feet, he pulled the condom from his pocket, unzipped his fly and put it on. The moon peeked through the trees to give him a glimpse of her lying sprawled on the blanket in reckless abandon.

Her hair fanned out in disarray and her breasts quiv-ered with each ragged breath. The moonlight caught the sheen of passion on her silken thighs. She'd given her-self without hesitation, like some wild thing he'd met in the woods. He rejoiced in her total surrender, even if it was only for tonight.

As he knelt beside her, she reached for his hand and laced her fingers through his. He had just enough light to see the gleam in her eyes and her knowing smile. Realization hit him with the force of a lightning strike.

She got it. She understood his urge to celebrate with raw, uncivilized sex in the woods because she knew how rarely an artist's creation turned out exactly right. His world shifted. He'd never shared that depth of un-derstanding with anyone.

Taking her other hand, he slid his fingers through hers and pressed their joined hands against the blanket as he moved between her thighs. His body blocked the moonlight, but it didn't matter whether he could see her eyes. Slowly pushing his cock into her warmth, he felt a connection that took his breath away.

Maybe this wouldn't be the hard-driving, no-holds-barred experience he'd anticipated, after all. He loved her with long, sure strokes. Each time he locked his body against hers, he paused a moment to breathe, to treasure the beauty of being so intimately joined with Sapphire, the woman of his dreams.

Her nipples brushed his chest with each deliberate thrust and her fingertips pressed into the backs of his hands. He didn't want this to end but his climax edged closer. Giving in to the demands of his cock, he gradually increased the pace.

Ah, that was good, too. The sweet friction seemed more intense than before. She moaned and tightened around him, sending shock waves through his entire body. He pumped faster. Every sensual pleasure was amplified—the earthy smell of sex, the liquid sound of each stroke, the satin touch of her thighs as she raised her hips and wrapped her legs around his waist.

They were in shadow, but if he closed his eyes, he saw color everywhere—the red of desire, the blue of trust, the yellow of creativity, the green of hope and the entire rainbow that was love. The first ripple of her climax rolled over his cock and he bore down. Panting, he rode the crest of her orgasm and claimed his own. Their cries mingled in the cool night air.

Later, after he'd carried her back to the truck and helped her dress, they smiled and kissed, but no significant words were spoken. He didn't plan to say them now. He knew what he knew and she had to be aware they'd crossed a line.

He'd see how things went for the next two days. He was scheduled to leave for Cody on Sunday. If he hadn't found a time before then to make his case, then he'd make it on Sunday. He wasn't leaving town until he'd said what was in his heart.

NOW SHE'D GONE and done it. She'd fallen in love with him. But she couldn't tell him so or he'd say it back to her. Then they'd have a problem because she didn't know what to do about this love situation.

Lucky for her, conversation wasn't necessary for the rest of the night. When they were both naked, they managed to communicate quite well without saying a word. They made love again after they reached her house, and making love was the only way to describe it. They were now incapable of just having sex. Then they slept like a couple of hibernating bears until her alarm went off.

They fooled around in the shower before leaving the house and she managed to enjoy the heck out of that without blurting out something stupid. She sensed he was waiting for her to say it because she was the one with hang-ups about artists. She was counting on their busy schedule to keep her from making a huge mistake. Once those three little words were out, there was no taking them back.

She suggested they drive separately to the Art Barn because she had lots of errands today. That was very true, but she also needed some privacy so she could think. That didn't work out quite as smoothly as she'd imagined, because they left together and the lack of traffic at that hour meant his truck stayed in her rearview mirror the whole way.

At every light, he was right behind her, and when he caught her looking in the mirror, he smiled. That smile jacked up her pulse every damn time. But just because she'd fallen in love with him, didn't mean she had to do anything about it.

If she hadn't gone out to Thunder Mountain Ranch with him, she might have avoided the love part. That fateful decision was totally on her because she'd been all set to stay home until she'd looked at those wolves.

She didn't regret being there when he'd presented the sculpture to Rosie, though.

She didn't regret anything. Their moment of clarity in the woods would be a cherished memory forever. Two people seldom communicated on that level, and because of that, she might always love Grady Magee.

That didn't mean she was ready to take a chance on him as a life partner, not with her track record. For all she knew, his glaring faults were obvious but she was too blinded by love, artistic bonding and great sex to see them. Once he left and took his powerful charisma with him, she might realize how wrong they were for each other.

She doubted that he was viewing it that way, though. For that matter, he might be blind to her faults, too. The world was full of miserable people who leaped into commitment in the heat of the moment and then had to figure out how to extricate themselves from bad situations.

This week observing Grady making a sculpture for his beloved foster mother was bound to make him seem like a hero. No wonder she'd fallen for him after last night's emotional episode. No wonder she'd had the lovemaking experience of her life afterward.

So her private thinking time had brought her around to that hot topic and she arrived at the Art Barn feeling restless and aroused. She might as well have had him sitting in the passenger seat of her truck. At least then she could have glanced over to admire how his faded jeans hugged his thighs.

George's tan truck was in the parking lot, which was a good thing. She'd be less tempted to steal a kiss or ten from Grady. She shut off the engine, grabbed her purse and hopped down.

Grady pulled in next to her and got out. She waited for him and tried hard not to look besotted as she watched him approach. From the way he was staring at her, she almost expected him to kiss her before they walked in.

But he surprised her. "Before I forget, your left tail-light is out."

"It is?" She'd thought he'd been intent on her mouth and he'd been focused on her truck's taillight.

"Yeah, and I want credit for not kissing you out here in broad daylight."

She gazed at him. "Admirable."

"Better not push it, though. I'm weakening."

So was she. "Let's go in."

He nodded and fell into step beside her. "Unless you think I'll spook Fred, I'd like to help with the ferals this morning so I can see the progress you've made."

"I'd like you to see it, too. It's possible he'll revert back to the way he was, but let's find out what happens if you're there."

"Sounds good. I'll need to feed Gandalf and pay attention to him, so just holler when you're ready."

"I will." Because her mind was a traitor to the cause, she immediately remembered how she'd hollered last night during that episode in the woods. So had he. They'd probably frightened the wildlife.

After they got inside, George poked his head out from his workspace. "Hope you don't mind, Grady, but I fed your cat. He's back here hanging out with me."

Grady laughed. "I'm sure he gave you the pitiful face."

"Yeah, he did. I didn't think you'd mind if I put some food in his bowl. Oops, here he comes. Guess he loves you best, after all. Fickle cat."

"If you had tuna, you'd be golden," Grady said as Gandalf trotted toward them, tail in the air.

"Go ahead and love on him." Sapphire watched as the cat loped up and marveled at the transformation. With his coat brushed and his manner confident, he looked like a whole different animal. "I'll fill the bowls."

"Okay." Grady crouched down and started talking to Gandalf while giving him a full-body massage.

Sapphire forced herself to turn away and go about her business. Creative men were her weakness. Being kind to animals added a whole new layer to their appeal. If she wanted to blame anyone for the fiasco of falling in love with Grady, she could probably start with the cat.

She filled the bowls with dry food and called for Grady. He appeared in the kitchen doorway with Gandalf riding on his shoulder. "He wants to go, but I've told him he can't."

"Better not. No telling what would happen. We don't know if he was accepted by the colony. I'd advise keeping him inside until you leave for Cody." She was proud of the matter-of-fact way she said that, as if his departure was just another event that would take place in the course of this weekend.

Grady gave her a long look, though, as if trying to decipher her comment. "Good advice," he said at last. He set Gandalf on the floor. "Stay here, buddy. I'll be back in a little bit."

"You'll have to watch him as we go out." She was amused by Grady's assumption the cat would obey a command. "He might try to slip through the door. You're leaving with food. He might want to know what that's all about."

"I'll watch him." Grady picked up two sets of stacked bowls. Sure enough, Gandalf followed him as he walked to the front door. "I said *stay*."

The cat gazed up at him, tail twitching.

"I mean it, Gandalf."

George came down the aisle toward them. "I'll hold him while you go out there. I agree with Sapphire. He's gonna want to follow you and he shouldn't be out there. He wasn't born to be wild." When he scooped up the cat, Gandalf wiggled in his arms. "Better go before he scratches me."

"Thanks, George." Sapphire opened the door and they both made it out before Gandalf got loose.

"He could learn to stay." Grady paused to glance back at the closed door. "He just hasn't been trained."

"I suppose if you worked on it long enough. I've seen trained house cats, but they're not like dogs, who will do anything to please you."

"It would have been a whole lot easier if I'd stayed inside with him."

"It would, but I'm glad you wanted to come out here. You're the only one who knows how much I've wanted to domesticate Fred. I'm hoping he's there waiting for us."

"Really?"

"We'll see in a second." They rounded the corner of the barn and, sure enough, Fred sat with the others, his attention fixed on the spot where he knew she'd appear. Her heart melted. "There he is."

"I'll be damned. He doesn't seem like the same cat."

"I know. I really think you and Gandalf had an effect on him."

"Gandalf will be happy to hear that."

That made her smile. She studied at him. "You're so—"

"In love with you." He turned his head and met her gaze.

Her heart hammered and she felt slightly dizzy. "Grady..."

"I swore I wouldn't say it before you did. You don't

have to respond at all. It'd be better if you didn't. My timing sucks. But the words have been lodged in my throat for hours. I was ready to choke on them. So they're out there. Now let's get these cats fed." He broke eye contact and set his bowls on the ground.

She did the same and they both dropped to their knees to watch the cats. Or rather, Grady did that while she looked at Grady. His throat moved in a slow swallow and a muscle tightened in his jaw. He'd nicked himself while hurrying to shave after their sexy time in the shower. She wanted to lean over and kiss that spot but she didn't dare.

Instead she forced herself to turn away and stare at the cats lined up in front of them, although her thoughts were still on the Stetson-wearing man beside her. *So in love with you.* She contemplated what would happen if she admitted to loving him back. He'd expect that to change things, to pave the way for them to be together.

If anything, it was exactly the opposite. Loving him meant she was in that addled state that allowed people to screw up their lives. She wasn't thinking straight, and oh, by the way, neither was he.

In the three weeks since they'd met and fallen in lust, he'd built an elaborate fantasy involving her. Yes, they had a great time together and her artist's soul communed with his. That was nice, but it didn't guarantee happiness. Some issue was lurking in the background waiting to zap them with a dose of cold, hard reality. She just didn't know what it was.

The cats finished their meal and began grooming themselves, except for Fred, who sat and gazed at Sapphire. Snow White came over for a scratch and Sapphire gave her attention while continuing to watch Fred. When Snow White wandered away, Sapphire blinked at

Fred. He blinked back. Slowly, she extended her hand in his direction.

He looked at her outstretched hand. Then he stood. His body tense and poised for flight, he gradually inched toward her.

She held her breath. Tail twitching, he edged close enough to sniff her hand. She stayed as still as possible, although her hand shook from the effort of keeping it in that position. Then, to her astonishment, he rubbed his head against her curved fingers.

Her gasp of surprise startled him and he dashed away. Halfway to the woods he paused and looked back. A second more and he was gone, disappearing into the shadows.

With a sigh, she glanced over at Grady. "I scared him."

His smile was tinged with sadness. "It happens."

"But I'll get there."

He nodded. "You will, and that gives me hope."

She gazed at him in confusion.

"I think I know why you're so attached to Fred."

"Oh?"

"He's a lot like you."

15

GRADY WISHED HE'D kept his mouth shut. His ill-timed declaration of love affected his interaction with Sapphire for the rest of the day. She was wary and skittish whenever their paths crossed. Just like Fred.

Oh, she loved him, too. He didn't doubt that for a minute. But now he was paying for the actions of those other guys who'd professed undying love and later kicked her in the chops. She believed he might be capable of the same thing.

The day would have been more awkward if they hadn't both been busy getting ready for the fund-raiser. In checking his materials for the cougar, he noticed he was missing a couple of things. He ended up calling around town to find them and eventually driving to a junkyard outside town. He made it back just in time for his scheduled TV interview, which would be part of the nightly news to ramp up attendance.

Sapphire's efficiency was something to behold as she made sure everything on her list was accomplished by either her or one of the other co-op members. Rented tables and chairs were picked up, mini lights were hung throughout the barn, and every stall was dusted and swept.

A velvet rope strung down the middle of the barn aisle was designed to facilitate traffic flow, and the same style of rope cordoned off each stall so that visitors would keep a respectful distance from the artists at work. Sapphire and Arlene painted a large banner to hang across the front entrance.

Grady found out from George that Rangeland Roasters, a local coffee shop, had volunteered to set up a cart outside next to the entrance. Scruffy's had agreed to operate a cash bar on the other side and offer happy-hour munchies. All profits from food and beverage sales would go to the shelter. Stan Ferguson's jazz trio was playing free of charge.

"She's thought of everything." George folded his arms and glanced around. "This event wouldn't have happened without her. Hell, the co-op wouldn't have happened without her. I wouldn't have become friends with you, either, come to think of it. Gonna miss working across the aisle from you when this is over."

"I'll miss you, too. This has been a great experience." Now that he had so little time left here, he wasn't ready for it to end, and not only because of Sapphire. He'd enjoyed the camaraderie of artists working under the same roof.

But his studio at home was better suited to his needs, and living in the same town as Liam and his mom was important. They'd been through a lot together. Rosie and Herb meant a great deal to him, but his mom and Liam anchored his world.

"I hope you'll pay us a visit now and then," George said. "If this fund-raiser does as well as we hope, Sapphire might decide to organize another one next year.

I'm sure she'd love to have you be a part of it." He peered down the aisle where she was adjusting the velvet rope. "Isn't that right, Sapphire?"

She glanced up and tucked her mane of auburn hair behind her ear. "What's that?"

"If we do another fund-raiser next year, we should invite Grady to be a part of it."

"Of course." Her answer was cheerful but her body stiffened.

Grady wondered if she'd figured on his making friends who would want to see him again. He'd become an honorary member of the co-op, whether she wanted him to be or not.

"But remember," she continued, "he's getting more famous by the day. That adds responsibilities to an artist's schedule, so he might not be able to spare the time."

George turned his all-knowing Santa smile on Grady. "You won't get too highfalutin for us, will you, son?"

"Sure won't." He looked over at Sapphire. "If you have another event like this, you'd damn well better invite me or I'll have to crash the party."

"Duly noted."

"There you go." George chuckled. "I knew you'd developed a good opinion of this outfit. Well, we'd better quit jawing and get back to work before Sapphire cracks her whip." He winked at Grady and retreated into his area.

"And I might, too." She made one last adjustment to the rope. "I have high hopes for this, both for raising money and for giving us exposure prior to the holidays. It's not too early for people to start thinking about Christmas presents." She called out to George. "Should you put on the suit tomorrow night?"

George came back into the aisle. "Too obvious. And it's only August."

"You're right. Forget the suit, but could we make up some cute signs with a subtle Christmas motif to put in each work area to remind people that original art makes a great gift?"

George nodded. "I'd go along with that."

"I'll talk to Arlene." She started to leave.

"Wait a sec," George said. "Are we all having dinner at Scruffy's tonight? We talked about it a couple of weeks ago."

"We did, and I completely forgot. Do you want to?" She directed the question to George and didn't look directly at Grady.

"I think it would be good for all of us to have some drinks and loosen up. We've been working pretty hard lately."

"You're right."

Grady could almost see the wheels turning. Loosening up in a social setting was probably the last thing she wanted to do. Chances were excellent that everyone would figure out he was in love with her. And vice versa.

But George was pushing for it. "Eloise asked this morning if it was still on. It's been a while since I danced with my wife."

"Then we should do it. I'll see who else is free." Sapphire started to leave again.

"FYI, I'm free," Grady called after her because he couldn't resist.

"That's the spirit." George clapped him on the shoulder. "Work hard, party harder. That's my motto."

She turned back to gaze at them. "Well, okay, then. That's four of us confirmed. I'll check with the others."

He watched her walk away.

"So have you told her yet?"

Grady glanced at George. "Told her what?"

"That you're in love with her."

He hesitated and decided there was no point in trying to fool George. "Yep."

"She's gun-shy. Dated some real losers."

"So I've heard."

George squeezed his arm. "She's got a winner in you."

"Thanks for that, but how can you tell I'm not like the rest of them? You've only known me a few days."

"Number one, I've lived a lot more years than you and Sapphire and I've become a pretty good judge of character. Number two, and this might sound a little out there, but I see honesty in your work. Some artists are technically amazing but their work isn't honest. I trust someone who does honest work. Does that make any sense?"

"It does, and I can't think of higher praise than that." Grady's throat tightened. "Thank you."

"You're most welcome. Her work is honest, too, which is why you two get along so well. But she's young and she's been burned. Give her time."

He blew out a breath. "I will."

"She might need a lot of it."

"I know, and there's no guarantee she'll ever come around."

"Life doesn't come with guarantees, son. Only possibilities."

POSSIBILITIES WHIRLED IN Grady's mind as he grabbed a chair beside Sapphire's at Scruffy's. The group had pushed two tables together and, in the scramble for seats, Grady made sure he was in the right place at the right time so he could spend the evening next to her.

They'd driven from the Art Barn in separate vehicles and would have to drive back to her house that way, too. It wasn't his favorite way to do things, especially tonight, when he wanted to stick close. So he'd be damned if he'd sit at the opposite end of the table from her.

Pitchers of beer were ordered and everyone filled their mugs, including Sapphire. Grady was glad to see that. She could have decided not to risk getting too happy, all things considered. But she'd worked hard and deserved to let go a little. Talk was lively around the table and many toasts were made.

The food was slow in coming but more pitchers of beer arrived. Grady had grabbed a fast-food lunch that hadn't been very filling, so he didn't take any more beer when the pitcher went around. He wanted to be fully functioning so he could dance with Sapphire. The band was playing a slow number he liked, so he decided to ask her.

"Okay." She gave him a bright smile, maybe a little too bright.

He led her out to the floor and drew her into his arms.

She nestled against him and gazed into his eyes. "Grady, I'm drunk."

"Already?"

She nodded.

"But we just got here a little while ago." He pulled her in a little tighter because she didn't seem very steady on her feet.

"I forgot to eat today."

"Uh-oh. How much beer have you had?"

"Not sure."

He stopped dancing and guided her to the edge of the dance floor. "What do you want to do?"

"Go home."

"I'll take you. But you need food." He tried to remember what was in her refrigerator. "Do you have eggs?"

"Yes."

"Bread?"

"Yes."

"That'll work." Scrambled eggs and toast usually helped soak up the booze. Sliding an arm around her waist, he walked her back to the table. "Sapphire's not feeling good. I'm going to drive her home."

Amid a chorus of "Feel better soon" comments, he grabbed her purse and maneuvered her out the door.

The sight of the parking lot must have reminded her that she'd driven here. "My truck."

"No worries. We'll pick it up tomorrow."

She nodded. "Thanks."

"Welcome." He got her over to his truck and lifted her into the passenger seat. He had to buckle the seat belt for her.

"I'm an idiot," she murmured.

"No, you just got distracted by all you had to do and forgot to eat." He squeezed her shoulder before closing the door and going around to the driver's side. When he climbed in, she'd leaned her head back and closed her eyes. "Are you okay? Do you feel sick to your stomach?"

"No." She sighed. "Just embarrassed."

"There's nothing to be embarrassed about. These things happen. I'll take you home and make you some food." He shoved the key in the ignition.

"I love you, Grady."

He looked over at her. She hadn't moved and her eyes

were still closed. He wanted to bang his head against the steering wheel. She'd said it, but only because she was plastered. "I know." He started the engine and left the parking lot.

On the drive back he watched the road for bumps and potholes. If she was embarrassed about being drunk, she'd be mortified if she barfed in his truck. He managed to get her home and into the house without incident. Then he left her on the couch while he rummaged around in the kitchen.

He used up all the eggs she had because he was pretty damned hungry himself. He toasted several slices of bread, too. Then he found herbal tea in the cupboard and made some of that.

When it was all ready, he went into the living room. At first he thought she was asleep. He stood there a moment wondering if he should wake her.

As he debated, she opened her eyes. "It smells wonderful."

"Think you're up to eating something?"

"Yes." Taking a deep breath, she sat up.

He held out his hand. "Then dinner is served."

She smiled and put her hand in his. "You're the best. I owe you one."

"No, you don't." He pulled her up and into his arms. "You took in my cat, which was a major pain in the ass. Bringing you home and fixing you dinner doesn't come close to paying that bill." He gave her a quick kiss but didn't linger. She needed food more than kisses. "Let's eat."

"Let's do." She looked much steadier as she walked into the kitchen and sat down. "Aw. You made tea."

"I'm handy that way." He took the seat across from

her so he had a better view and could judge how she was doing. "I'd advise you to eat slowly."

"I will." She picked up her fork. "You sound experienced in this matter."

"Let's just say the guys I worked with in Alaska enjoyed their booze, especially during those long winter nights."

"I'll bet." She took a bite of her eggs, chewed and swallowed. "Good job on these. Not too dry and not too runny."

"Rosie taught me. She required every boy to take a turn in the kitchen, either helping her cook or helping her clean up afterward. She said our future wives would appreciate it."

"I'm sure they will." She kept her eyes on her plate as she ate more of the eggs.

Maybe he shouldn't have mentioned that, but Rosie's comment came back to him often when he messed around in the kitchen. He tucked into his eggs. They were excellent, if he did say so himself.

She finished off her eggs at a leisurely pace. "I'm feeling much better." She munched on a piece of toast. "Fixing this was a really good idea and the tea is perfect."

"Thanks." He had a feeling she had more to say.

"Maybe it's a good thing that I drank too much beer and had to come home."

"Maybe it was." He wished she was leading up to a seduction but nothing about her voice or her body language suggested that.

"We need to talk."

Bingo. He sighed. "I suppose so."

Pushing her plate away, she folded her arms on the

table and stared at him. "This morning you said you're in love with me."

"Which I am. Head over heels." Saying it made his heart beat faster.

Her breath hitched but she kept her arms calmly folded. "A little while ago I said that I love you."

"I won't hold you to that. You were—"

"You can hold me to that."

For one glorious moment he was the happiest guy in the world.

"But people in love aren't rational. They do stupid things like make promises they'll never keep."

The bubble burst. "Sometimes." He regarded her steadily. "Other times they know exactly what they're promising and are faithful to those promises."

"How do I know you would be?"

"You don't. You'd have to take it on faith."

"And if I can't do that?"

He shrugged. "We have a problem. Which I know we do. You're afraid to trust me and get slam-dunked again. I don't blame you."

She studied him over the rim of her teacup. Then she drained the contents. "What if I did take it on faith that you'll be loyal and true forever? What then?"

"We're getting ahead of ourselves."

"Not really. I have a feeling you've mapped this out the same way you make a sketch before you create a sculpture."

She really did know him, which was both thrilling and terrifying. "Ultimately, I'd want you to move down to Cody. There's more than enough room for you to share my studio on the ground level of the barn and Liam will be vacating the top floor within a month or so."

"I was right. You have thought this through."

"Of course I have. I'm in love with you."

"So you'd expect me to relocate?"

"It makes the most sense."

She flushed. "To you, maybe, but what about Amethyst and my folks? What about the co-op?"

"I've considered all that." He could see she wanted to argue the point and he held up a hand. "Honestly, I have. But the co-op needs you more than you need the co-op." He leaned forward. "Sapphire, your pottery is dynamite. I've made some valuable connections in the art world and you're welcome to them. Let George run the co-op. He'd do a fine job."

"So I'm supposed to leave my family—"

"I don't suggest that lightly, but you and Amethyst won't live together forever. As for your folks, maybe you do need to be in the same town. If so, we'd have to figure that out. Maybe we can come up with a decent compromise. But after having Liam and me in foster care for two years, my mother needs to keep us close. The truth is, we need that, too."

Her gaze softened. "I can understand why."

"Sapphire, I'm asking you to give us a chance."

"You're asking a whole lot more than that. You want me to leave my family and the co-op I've created. You're asking me to move in with you after we've only known each other for a few days. Talk about a leap of faith, especially considering—"

"Damn it, I know! You've had some rotten experiences! How I wish I could somehow wipe the slate clean and start fresh."

"You can't."

"I'm becoming increasingly aware of that." He looked at her. "Am I beating my head against a stone wall?" He thought of George's comment that changing her mind could take quite a while. For the first time he wondered if he had the patience.

Heartbreak shimmered in her turquoise eyes. "I do love you."

"And that's the toughest part of this! I know you do, and yet—"

"Because I love you, I'm telling you to give up on me. Don't stick around waiting to see if I'll change my mind. I won't leave you dangling like that. I can't make that leap of faith you're asking for. Let me go, Grady."

His heart stalled. "You really mean that."

"I do. We're done."

Despair howled within him, but he managed to sit there as if his world hadn't suddenly imploded. "Then I should probably take my stuff and move into the Art Barn for the night."

"You could, but then I'd be stranded here."

"Oh."

"Stay here tonight, Grady. It'll be okay."

Of course it wasn't. He agreed that sleeping on her couch was stupid, and once he was in her bed, they made love. And made love again. Each time it was like a dagger through his heart, but he couldn't lie next to her without taking her in his arms.

The next morning they moved through their routine like zombies. He packed up all his stuff because he knew he couldn't spend another night like this. After the fund-raiser he and Gandalf would hit the road.

16

SAPPHIRE HAD ALREADY ranked Saturday as one of the most miserable days of her life and it wasn't over yet. By the end of the night it could earn the top spot. She hoped the only people who knew that were Grady and her mother.

Her mom had come looking for her while her dad was setting up his sound equipment and had found her in the kitchen crying. She'd convinced her mother that Grady wasn't at fault. If she hadn't, there would have been an ugly scene. Grady didn't deserve that just because he thought falling in love was the endgame.

Besides, the fund-raiser was off to a great start and much of the credit was his. The crowd had filled the parking lot long before the artists were scheduled to start. When she'd realized they might pack themselves into the barn and violate the fire code, she'd asked Herb to stand at the entrance and monitor the number of visitors going in.

Belatedly, she'd figured out that she shouldn't be one of the performing artists. As the person in charge of this event, she should be free to roam and make sure everything went smoothly. Fortunately, the director of the shelter offered to do that and Rosie said she'd help, too.

Ten minutes before showtime, Sapphire went inside and stopped at each work area to give hugs and encouragement. For some it was the first time they'd worked in front of an audience. She saved Grady for last.

He wore his work gloves and his goggles hung around his neck. A sketch of the cougar was tacked on the wall and the recycled metal pieces lay on the floor in a precise order. His steady gaze told her he was focused on the work and ready to begin, but he hadn't put up the velvet rope blocking access to his space.

She stepped inside but didn't move within touching distance. "Thank you for doing this."

His expression didn't change. "My pleasure."

"I guess you know there's a mob of people out there. I think the majority came to see you."

His chest heaved, the first sign of any emotion. "I'll do my best to give them a good show."

"I know you will. Good luck." She turned to go.

"Sapphire." His voice was edged with strain.

Heart pounding, she faced him.

"You know I'm planning to leave for Cody when this is over, right?"

"I figured that when you packed up this morning." Her voice quavered and she hated that. She forced herself to smile. "Especially when you took your toothbrush."

"I can stay an extra day if you need me to." Hope flickered in his brown eyes. "You'll have some massive cleanup. I'd be glad to help with it."

So tempting. But it would only prolong the pain. "Thank you for offering, but we can handle it. You and Gandalf have a long drive ahead of you."

His expression closed down again. "We do."

"Just don't leave without saying goodbye."

"Wouldn't dream of it."

"Okay." Taking a deep breath, she rounded the wall to her work area. A moment later his torch hissed to life.

The next few hours passed in a blur. She had her share of people come by to say hello and many stayed for several minutes to watch her progress on a large salad bowl. She'd lived in Sheridan all her life and had made a lot of friends.

But the evening belonged to Grady. He was more of a crowd-pleaser than she'd imagined he'd be. Because of his intense focus, she'd expected him to weld the piece without interacting with his audience, but instead he paused to answer questions in an easy, relaxed manner that noticeably charmed the onlookers.

She could talk and work at the same time, too, but it took far more concentration than when she could simply create without interruption. She assumed it cost Grady, too, and he was planning to drive to Cody afterward. Maybe she should ask him to stay, after all.

The results of the silent auction dramatically capped the proceedings. All the pieces brought a respectable price, but a wealthy couple from Jackson Hole paid a small fortune for Grady's cougar. Apparently, word had spread that far. The shelter would be funded for months on the basis of that single sale.

The director was ecstatic, and despite Grady's protests, she hugged his sweat-soaked body. He grinned and made jokes for the benefit of the television crew that had appeared for the final part of the event, but Sapphire saw the exhaustion in his eyes. She'd steal a moment and suggest he stay until morning. If that was in her bed, so be it. She didn't want him risking his neck on the road.

Gradually, the crowd dispersed and George started organizing the cleanup crew. "You're excused, Grady," he said. "You, too, Sapphire. You both look like you've been rode hard and put away wet. Go get some rest."

Grady started packing his tools. "Thanks, George, but I'm heading out."

George blinked. "Tonight?"

"Yeah." Grady smiled at him. "Tons of work at home. Might as well get back to it."

George glanced over at Sapphire. "See if you can talk him out of that plan, okay?"

"I will."

"You're probably the only one who can convince him not to do something foolish." He turned to Grady. "For what it's worth, son, don't be an idiot."

Grady laughed. "Too late."

Shaking his head, George walked away.

"He's right," Sapphire said. "Don't leave."

He lifted his head, his gaze sharp. "Do you mean you don't want me to leave now or you don't want me to leave at all?"

Her breath caught.

"I see from your expression that this is a temporary request, not a permanent one. In that case, I'd prefer to go now." He went back to putting everything away.

"But you're exhausted."

"I've been exhausted before." He closed up a box. "Matter of fact, exhaustion can be a cleansing experience. Clears the mind."

"Meaning what?" Maybe he'd realized that he wasn't ready to make a commitment, either.

He stopped packing and looked at her. "I want you in my life. I believe we'd have a great time together. Not perfect, but pretty damned wonderful. You told me not to hang around and wait for you, so I won't do that. But Liam is moving out of the loft of our barn in October. I'm gonna hope like hell that you decide to move in."

Her pulse raced. "Grady, I already said—"

"I know exactly what you said. It's etched in my brain. You're giving up because you don't trust either of us to get this right. I, on the other hand, trust both of us. If you change your mind, you know where to find me."

"No, I don't. Not that I'll drive down there, but—"

"Just stop anywhere and ask. They'll give you directions." His expression softened. "You really should go home and get some rest, like George said. You look wiped."

She lifted her chin. "I'll go home when I decide to go home."

"Independent woman." He sighed. "Damn, I promised myself I wouldn't do this." Abruptly pulling her into his arms, he kissed her. His lips came down hard on hers as if he needed to vent his frustration, but eventually, his mouth gentled and then he slowly released her. "Please get out of here. It'll be tough enough to go as it is, but we both know I have to."

She dragged in air. "You don't have to go tonight."

"Yes, I do." A tender light glowed in his eyes. "The sooner I leave, the sooner you'll start to miss me. Now take off."

"All right." She turned and walked away because that was the smart thing to do. Yes, she might be crying right now, and yes, she'd miss him like crazy for a while, but she'd get over it at some point. Once she did, she'd be proud of herself for dodging a bullet.

A MONTH AND a half later she was still telling herself that and waiting for the persistent ache in her heart to go away. The progress with Fred helped. Everyone had agreed to put his food dish inside the barn door so he'd become used to eating apart from the others.

He wouldn't let anyone pet him, but he was willing to stroke his face against an outstretched hand. Project Fred seemed to be working. He might become a barn cat yet. After Gandalf's departure, they all agreed they needed one.

She'd just finished the feeding routine one weekday morning and was washing the bowls when someone rapped on the front door of the Art Barn. It wasn't officially open yet, but she never wanted to pass up a chance to sell some art. She dried her hands and went to see who'd shown up at seven thirty in the morning.

Rosie stood on the other side of the door. "Have you finished with the kitties?" She glanced around as if expecting cats to be prowling around the parking lot.

"Yes, but how did you know I would be here doing that?"

"Grady told me. Do you have a few minutes?"

"Sure, sure! Come in!" Grady had told her? When? She ushered Rosie into the office and offered her a chair and coffee. She politely declined the coffee but took the chair. It was the only one other than the desk chair, so Sapphire leaned against the desk rather than sitting behind it.

"You probably wonder what on earth I'm doing here." Rosie settled into the chair.

"You're always welcome, but yes, I'm curious."

"Herb and I drove down to visit Liam and Grady last weekend."

Sapphire's pulse leaped. She'd had no word from him, but then, he hadn't said he'd communicate with her.

"I wanted to see the little house Hope and Liam are

moving into and I took Grady an apple pie. He loves my apple pies, and I wanted to do something nice for him after he made those wolves for me."

"The sculpture! I was supposed to help you with the lighting. Do you still need me to?" That couldn't be the reason for this early morning visit. A phone call would have been sufficient.

"Damon and Phil rigged up something, although it might need tweaking."

"Let me know if you need me to come out."

Rosie met her gaze. "I was hesitant to ask you because I thought you and Grady had a big fight."

"A fight? No, not at all."

"He said the same thing. I hope you don't mind, but I talked him into explaining the issues."

Sapphire took a shaky breath. Rosie was in matchmaking mode. "He told me you wanted to see your boys settled, but I'm afraid that in this case—"

"Would you be willing to hear me out?"

What could she say? "Of course."

"If I understand this correctly, you don't think a few days together gave you enough information to risk throwing in your lot with Grady."

"That's right." She steeled herself for an argument.

"Good for you."

She stared at Rosie. "Excuse me?"

"Sure, there are times when a few days are enough, but after your experiences with bad boyfriends, you'd have to be crazy to follow Grady down to Cody after such a short acquaintance. He was naive to think you would."

She sighed in relief. "Thank you! I expected a lecture about not trusting in the power of love."

"Not my style." Rosie leaned forward. "But I was a

mother to that boy for two years and I've been a part of his life ever since. I have a strong feeling you two belong together, so I'm here to give you the information you need so you can put your faith in Grady Magee."

GRADY HAD TOLD himself not to pin his hopes on Rosie's visit with Sapphire. Rosie could make him do nearly anything in the world, but that didn't mean she'd have the same effect on Sapphire. The plan made sense, though. Rosie had proposed giving Sapphire a crash course in all things Grady.

When he thought of the pranks he'd pulled during his time at the ranch, he hoped she'd leave out those episodes. Her goal was getting Sapphire down to Cody, so she'd likely emphasize his good side. But if she made him sound too angelic, that would seem suspicious, too. He'd have to trust her to get the right mix. Her text after the visit was cryptic. Talked to Sapphire. We'll see.

He texted a quick thank-you. Then he got to work because it was the only thing he'd found that would block out the intense yearning he'd dealt with since leaving Sheridan. Watching Liam feather his love nest with Hope certainly hadn't helped, although he was happy for them. The little house located a short walk from the barn was in the last stages of renovation and was in good enough shape for Liam and Hope to move in. The wedding was set for November.

Working like a demon had put Grady ahead of schedule, so he could make a wedding present for Hope and Liam. He didn't have to cover it every night now that Liam had moved out, which was helpful. The piece was a challenge because it was unlike anything he'd attempted.

No wildlife was involved. Instead he'd created a river

raft to represent Liam, but rather than being filled with people, the raft was loaded with books. Hope was an author and this was how Grady saw their partnership— Liam as the raft keeping Hope's dream afloat.

He was deep into it one afternoon when he heard someone pull up outside. So did Gandalf, who'd been asleep on top of his cat tree. He lifted his head and stared in the direction of the front door.

The cat's presence was bittersweet. Grady loved having him around, but he also served as a reminder of Sapphire. Gandalf was probably sick of hearing Sapphire's name come up constantly in their daily conversations.

"I sincerely doubt it's her," Grady said to the cat, "so don't get your hopes up, okay? Unless it's her, we're not opening the door. We don't let random folks come barging in when we're working. You should know that by now."

Gandalf's answering meow was sharp and to the point. He clearly wanted Grady to investigate. He was a social cat and loved visitors a lot more than Grady did.

"Oh, all right." He shut down the torch and took off his gloves and goggles. "I'll check to see who's out there, but if it's tourists, they don't get a tour. I'm finally getting those books sitting in the raft to look right."

He glanced out the window and nearly had a heart attack. Sapphire's purple truck sat in front of the barn. If this worked out, he might need to make Rosie another sculpture.

Breathing was an effort as he unlocked the double doors, stepped outside and closed the doors behind him to keep Gandalf from running out. Then he raked his fingers through his damp hair and shivered as the cool air hit his sweaty body. She'd claimed to like him covered in sweat.

She climbed out of the truck and he gobbled up the sight of her like a man dying of starvation. Sunlight gleamed in her wild auburn hair, which was caught back on one side with an elaborate clip. She'd worn the embroidered jeans he liked, but he'd never seen the colorful patchwork jacket. He remembered the earrings, though, the ones that dangled to her shoulders. As always, she knocked him out.

But instead of going to her, he hooked his thumbs in his belt loops and waited for her to come to him. She'd driven down here, which was a good sign, but he didn't know what that meant. Maybe she'd been in the area and had decided to stop by. Maybe she'd found something he'd left at her house and was here to return it.

She shut the door of the truck and walked toward him without anything in her hands—no purse, no package, no gift. Just her.

He drew in a breath. "Hey, Sapphire."

"Hey, Grady." She stopped several feet away. "How's Gandalf?"

"Good."

"Glad to hear it." She paused before continuing. "I guess you know Rosie came to see me."

"Her idea."

"But you approved it?"

"Absolutely." He looked into her eyes and tried to read her emotions. Couldn't do it.

"She really loves you."

"I really love her."

"She told me quite a bit about you."

"Mostly good, I hope."

"Mostly, but I heard about the firecrackers in the bathhouse and the spiked Christmas punch."

At least she hadn't made him out to be perfect. "I see."

"But I also heard about the puppy you rescued from a snowdrift and the time you slept in the barn to watch over a horse with colic. I heard about your loyalty to your brothers—Liam, of course, but all the foster brothers, too. She told me that you took on three guys at once because they called the Thunder Mountain boys losers."

"Almost got my ass kicked, too. Then Liam came along."

She nodded. "That's the other thing Rosie explained—the special bond between you and Liam. I respect that."

"Because you have a sister." Maybe she was here to tell him she wouldn't leave Sheridan for the same reason he didn't want to leave Cody.

"I do, and we're close, but...it's not the same, Grady. I get that now."

He held his breath, afraid to hope.

She stepped closer. "After the fund-raiser you issued me an invitation." She swallowed. "Is it still open?"

His heart beat so fast he prayed he wouldn't keel over. "It is."

"Then I'd like to accept."

"Thank God." He closed the distance in two strides and swept her into his arms. "Thank God, Sapphire." He looked into her turquoise eyes. "I've been dying down here."

She threaded her hands through his hair. "I've been dying up there. But I needed..."

He smiled. "A character reference?"

"Was that wrong of me?"

"No." He'd start kissing her any second, but for now, he was content to hold her and look into her eyes. "Rosie said you were smart to be cautious after what you'd been through. I thought you should instinctively know I was different."

"My heart did. But my head wasn't convinced."

"And now?"

"You've got all of me, Grady. Body and soul."

A surge of joy made him tremble. "I think this calls for a celebration."

"Champagne?"

"I was thinking of something more basic. Something more naked."

"But you've been welding. I don't want to interfere with—"

"It can wait." For the first time in three years, he abandoned his work without hesitation. It would be there after he'd made mind-blowing love to Sapphire, and miracle of miracles, so would she.

Epilogue

THE TWO-STORY HOUSE engulfed in flames was supposed to be vacant, but the Jackson Hole firefighters were well trained and none of them took that as gospel. Battling intense heat and smoke, they conducted a room-to-room search on the first floor and found nobody. The stairs were impassible, so Jake Ramsey went up a ladder to a second-floor window.

He ripped off the screen, broke the glass and climbed in. The first two rooms yielded nothing. One more to go and then he'd get the hell out of there. The floor could give way any second. In the third room, he found a kid curled up in a ragged sleeping bag. *Shit.*

The kid was unconscious but still breathing. Looked like a boy, judging from the haircut. Dragging him out of the sleeping bag, Jake hoisted him over his shoulder and returned to the window. He had to set him down while he broke out more of the glass.

He slung him over his shoulder again and started down. The kid was a lightweight, thank God. At the bottom a couple of guys took him and headed for the ambulance. Jake stared at the blazing house. The boy could have started it by leaving something turned on downstairs. Critters could have chewed on some wires in the attic.

Didn't really matter. What did matter was that no kid that age should be sleeping alone in an empty house. But it might have been the best option the boy could come up with. Jake knew all about that. He'd been that kid. If somebody hadn't caught him and turned him over to Child Protective Services, he never would have ended up at Thunder Mountain Ranch.

Later that night he stopped by the hospital to check on the kid. Sure enough, the terrified thirteen-year-old lived with an alcoholic, abusive father. According to the nurse on duty, the boy had told his dad that he was the most popular boy in the eighth grade. Since his friends supposedly kept begging him to spend the night, he'd had to rotate among the houses to keep everyone happy, which explained why he couldn't sleep at home. CPS had been called in.

A couple weeks later Chief Stanton summoned Jake into the office. "I know you've been worried about that kid you hauled out of the fire. Thought you'd be happy to know he's been placed in a real nice foster home."

Jake smiled in relief. "That's great news."

"Yeah, it is. I know the couple that took him and they're very nurturing. The boy should have a good Christmas for a change."

"I'm glad."

"Me, too. Could've been a whole lot worse ending for that kid. He's lucky."

Jake blew out a breath. "Yeah."

"Speaking of Christmas, you've worked every single one since you started. How'd you like to have it off this year?"

"I'd love it. How many days can you give me?"

"The twenty-third through the twenty-sixth is all I can spare, but that should at least give you enough time to head over to Sheridan."

"You bet it would. Thanks, Chief. This makes my day."

"You gotta work Thanksgiving, though."

"That's fine. No worries." He left the office whistling. He hadn't spent Christmas at Thunder Mountain in years, but he had great memories of the big tree, the great food and the holiday joy spread by his foster parents.

Then there was Amethyst Ferguson. She might have a gig somewhere else during the holidays, but he hoped not. His memories of Amethyst were more recent than his memories of Thunder Mountain. And a lot hotter.

He'd known she was performing in Jackson this past August, but he hadn't been able to catch a show until the last one. Afterward he'd sent a note backstage and she'd agreed to meet him for a drink for old times' sake. They'd had some epic make-out sessions in the back of his truck when they were in high school but he'd never had the nerve to go all the way.

They'd joked about the missed opportunity over drinks, jokes that had gradually taken on a seductive tone. She'd invited him up to her room at the resort so they could take advantage of this new opportunity. They'd taken advantage of it several times.

While they'd both had fun, they'd parted with the clear understanding that they'd shared a one-night stand. He'd been fine with that. His work was in Jackson and she was based in Sheridan. If her travels brought her back to Jackson, she'd let him know. Easy come, easy go.

Except that had been two months ago and he couldn't get her out of his mind. He'd ordered her albums and played them constantly. He remembered her scent, her voice, her touch and the delicious taste of her body.

He wasn't expecting a happily-ever-after. She didn't seem like the type. But if she happened to be in town, maybe they could give each other the gift of pleasure for the holidays. Sounded like a perfect Christmas present to him.

* * * * *

Want more of Vicki Lewis Thompson's
THUNDER MOUNTAIN BROTHERHOOD *series?*
Sparks are flying between Sapphire's artistic sister, Amethyst, and firefighter Jake Ramsey!
Watch for their story, coming December 2016, only from Harlequin Blaze!

#907 HANDLE ME
Uniformly Hot!
by Kira Sinclair
Military K-9 handler Ty Colson has been lusting after his best friend's little sister for years. Now she's finally letting him into her bed, but will she ever let him into her heart?

#908 TEMPTED IN THE CITY
NYC Bachelors
by Jo Leigh
Tony Paladino is a licensed contractor who is Little Italy royalty. Catherine Fox hires Tony to renovate her downtown property. The attraction is fierce—and mutual. Too bad they're complete opposites!

#909 HOT SEDUCTION
Hotshot Heroes
by Lisa Childs
Serena Beaumont has always been the good girl, the one who wants a husband and kids. But when she rents a room to a notorious player, Hotshot firefighter Cody Mallehan, she's tempted to be very, *very* bad.

#910 NO LIMITS
Space Cowboys
by Katherine Garbera
Astronaut Jason "Ace" McCoy wasn't expecting to add *rancher* to his job title. Will a few sizzling weeks with his ranch co-owner, Molly Tanner, tempt him to give up the stars and stay in the saddle for good?

REQUEST YOUR FREE BOOKS!
2 FREE NOVELS PLUS 2 FREE GIFTS!

HARLEQUIN®

Blaze®

red-hot reads!

*When military K-9 handler Ty Colson delivers retired
war dog Kaia to her new owner, Van Cantrell's head
wants nothing to do with the risk-hungry soldier
determined to return to the front lines. But her
body has other ideas...*

*Read on for a sneak preview of
HANDLE ME, the first of Kira Sinclair's
UNIFORMLY HOT! K-9 stories.*

"I suggest you do exactly what I plan on doing and forget
that night ever happened."

Van stared out at the neighborhood she called home. It
was quiet. Nice. Full of professionals and families. She
wanted to like it here, but honestly, it had never quite felt
like home.

She felt him way before she heard him. All that pent-
up tension and heat slipping over her skin like fingers,
caressing her into a reaction she didn't want to feel.

Ty didn't actually touch her, though. He didn't have to.

"You keep telling yourself that, princess," he whispered,
the soft puff of his breath tickling her ear. A shiver rolled
down her spine. He was too close not to notice.

He chuckled.

Van ground her teeth together, though she wasn't sure
if it was to bite back words or merely find another—
safer—outlet for all that pent-up energy.

"I remember every moment of that night," he

murmured, his words low and dangerous to her equilibrium.

"Highly unlikely considering how drunk you were."

His fingertips found the curve of her neck and slowly, devastatingly trailed across her skin. Goose bumps erupted in the wake of his touch, a telltale sign she was powerless to hide.

"I stopped drinking the minute we hit that tree house. I was sober as a judge by the time things got…heated."

"Ha!"

"The way you looked, naked, flushed with desire and spread out on that blanket, is something I'll never forget. Not as long as I live." Ty swept her hair over one shoulder, exposing the curve of her neck. The warm summer breeze ghosted over her, replaced almost immediately by the blazing heat of his mouth.

She whimpered. The sound simply escaped, uncontrollable and way too revealing.

No. "I can't do this," she said, the words coming out a strangled mess. "You're the reason my brother is dead. He never should have been in Afghanistan. He followed *you* into that life. My body might think you're God's gift to continuing the species, but my brain doesn't give a shit."

Ty's gaze hardened, his eyes like ice. In that moment she could see the ruthless, fearless, dangerous soldier that he'd become. "Take Kaia inside and be sure to give her plenty of water." His voice was flat. "I'll be back tomorrow."

*Don't miss HANDLE ME by Kira Sinclair,
available in September 2016 wherever Harlequin®
Blaze® books and ebooks are sold.*

www.Harlequin.com

HBEXP0816

Reading Has Its Rewards

Earn **FREE BOOKS!**

Register at **Harlequin My Rewards** and submit your Harlequin purchases from wherever you shop to earn points for free books and other exclusive rewards.

Plus submit your purchases from now till May 30th for a chance to win a $500 Visa Card*.

Visit **HarlequinMyRewards.com** today

MYR16R1